Because We Were In Love

OrangeBooks Publication

Smriti Nagar, Bhilai, Chhattisgarh - 490020

Website: **www.orangebooks.in**

First Edition, 2023

ISBN: 978-93-5621-853-6

Price: Rs.490.00

Printed in India

BECAUSE WE WERE IN LOVE

Let your love guide you

SANDEEP TIWARI

OrangeBooks Publication

www.orangebooks.in

Foreword

Love is a feeling that transcends time, space, and culture. It is the force that drives us, inspires us, and gives our lives meaning. Love can take many forms: the love between a parent and child, the love between friends, and the love between two people who have chosen to share their lives with each other.

The love between two people is a powerful force that has the ability to transform lives, change the world, and leave an indelible mark on our hearts. It is the love that has inspired the stories in this collection, **"Because We Were in Love."**

As a writer, I have always been fascinated by the power of love and the way it can transform lives. Love has the ability to inspire us, challenge us, and push us to be the best version of ourselves. It is this power of love that I have sought to capture in the stories in this collection.

Each of the stories in this collection is inspired by real-life love stories, stories of couples who have chosen to share their lives with each other and whose love has stood the test of time. These stories are not just about romantic love but about the power of love in all its forms. They are about the love between parents and children, the love between friends, and the love between partners who have chosen to build a life together.

What is remarkable about these stories is that they are all unique yet share a common thread: the power of love to transform lives. In each story, we see how love has the ability to bring people together, heal old wounds, and give our lives meaning and purpose.

But these stories are not just about love; they are also about the human experience. They are about the struggles, triumphs, and setbacks that we all face in our lives. They are about the moments that define us, the moments that challenge us, and the moments that ultimately shape our lives.

As I read through these stories, I was struck by the way in which they captured the essence of what it means to be human. They remind us that hope is always there, no matter what challenges we face or how difficult life may seem. There is always the possibility of love and the power of love to transform our lives.

In many ways, these stories are a testament to the resilience of the human spirit. They remind us that no matter what obstacles we face, no matter how impossible the odds may seem, love has the power to conquer all. Love has the power to heal, transform, and give us hope.

As you read through these stories, I hope you will be inspired by the power of love. I hope you will be reminded of the beauty and resilience of the human spirit, and of the hope that lies within all of us.

I would like to express my deepest gratitude to the couples who have shared their love stories with us. Your love, dedication, and commitment to each other have been the source of inspiration for these stories, and it is an honor to be able to share these stories with the world.

I would also like to express my gratitude to the writer who has brought these stories to life. Your talent, dedication, and hard work have made this collection possible, and it is a privilege to have worked with you.

Finally, I would like to thank the readers who have taken the time to read this collection. Your support and encouragement mean the world to us, and we hope these stories will touch your heart, inspire you, and remind you of the power of love.

In closing, I would like to leave you with these words: "Love is the most powerful force in the universe." It has the ability to transform lives, change the world, and leave an indelible mark on our lives.

Preface

Love, a pure and enchanting feeling, has been the subject of countless stories and poems throughout human history. It is a force that can move mountains, conquer obstacles, and make the impossible possible. From the love stories of Romeo and Juliet to Laila and Majnu, from Heer and Ranjha to Sohni and Mahiwal, love has always been a part of human culture and literature.

In this collection of love stories, we bring you tales of love that transcends time and space, tales of love that have stood the test of time, and tales of love that have inspired generations. Each story in this collection captures a unique aspect of love, from the joy of falling in love to the pain of heartbreak, from the struggle to keep love alive to the power of forgiveness.

These stories are not just about the love between two people but also about the love between family members, friends, and even strangers. They are stories of hope, courage, and resilience, reminding us that love can conquer all.

So, sit back and immerse yourself in these tales of love. Let them take you on a journey of emotions, and let them remind you of the power of love.

Love is a powerful emotion that has the ability to move mountains, break barriers, and conquer all. It is a force that has been written about for centuries, a source of inspiration for countless artists, writers, and musicians. Love has been the subject of countless stories, poems, and songs, each one unique in its portrayal of the human experience.

As an author, I have always been fascinated by the idea of love and the myriad of emotions that it evokes. It is this fascination that has led me to write this collection of love stories, **"Because We Were in Love."**

This collection is a celebration of love in all its forms, from the joy of falling in love to the pain of heartbreak, from the struggle to keep love alive to the power of forgiveness. Each story captures a unique aspect of love, and each one tells a tale of hope, courage, and resilience.

The stories in this collection are not just about romantic love but also about the love between family members, friends, and even strangers. They are stories that remind us of the beauty and power of human connection and of the importance of nurturing our relationships.

The title of this collection, **"Because We Were in Love,"** is a nod to the idea that love can be both the cause and the effect of our actions. Love is the reason why we do what we do, and it is also the result of our actions. It is a cycle that repeats itself over and over again, and it is this cycle that forms the backbone of the stories in this collection.

In these pages, you will find stories of ordinary people who find themselves in extraordinary situations and rise to the occasion with courage and grace. You will find stories of love that defy all boundaries, stories of love that endure through the toughest of times, and stories of love that inspire us to be better people.

As I wrote these stories, I was struck by the power of love and the transformative effect that it can have on our lives. Love has the ability to change us in ways that we never thought possible, to open our hearts to new experiences, and to help us see the world in a different light.

I hope these stories will inspire you to open your heart to love, embrace its power, and let it transform your life in ways that you never thought possible. I hope they will remind you that love is not just a feeling but a force that can change the world.

In closing, I would like to express my gratitude to all the people who have inspired me to write these stories, and to all the readers who will take the time to read them. It is my hope that **"Because We Were in Love"** will bring you joy, comfort, and inspiration, and it will remind you of the beauty and power of love in all its forms.

Acknowledgement

Writing a book is a solitary task, but bringing a book to life takes a village. With immense gratitude and humility, I acknowledge the people who have contributed to the creation of this collection of love stories, **"Because We Were in Love."**

First and foremost, I would like to express my deepest gratitude to my family, who have been my constant support system throughout the writing of this book. They have been a pillar of strength, encouragement, and love and have provided me the space and time to pursue my passion for writing. I could not have done this without them.

I am also deeply grateful to my friends, who have been my sounding board and my source of inspiration. Their unwavering support, encouragement, and feedback have been invaluable in shaping this book, and I am forever grateful to them.

I express my sincere gratitude to my editor, who has been instrumental in bringing this book to life. Your patience, guidance, and editorial expertise have been invaluable in shaping this collection of love stories.

I could not have asked for a better editor, and I am grateful for the opportunity to work with you.

I express my heartfelt thanks to the publishing team, who have worked tirelessly to bring this book to market. Your hard work, dedication, and professionalism have been the driving force behind this book, and I am grateful for the opportunity to work with such a talented and committed team.

I am also deeply grateful to the readers who will take the time to read this book. Your support and encouragement mean the world to me, and I hope these stories will touch your heart, inspire you, and remind you of the power of love.

Last but not least, I would like to acknowledge the people who have inspired the stories in this collection. To the couples whose love stories are the inspiration behind these tales, I express my sincere gratitude. Your love, dedication, and commitment to each other have been the source of inspiration for these stories, and I am honored to have been able to capture a small part of your love story in these pages.

I express my heartfelt thanks to the people who have been a part of my life and who have shown me the beauty and power of love. Your love, kindness, and support have been a constant source of inspiration, and I hope these stories will serve as a tribute to the love that you have shown me.

To my readers, I say thank you. Your support and encouragement have been the driving force behind this book, and I hope these stories will touch your heart, inspire you, and remind you of the power of love.

In closing, I would like to express my deepest gratitude to all the people who have been a part of this journey. Your support, encouragement, and love have been the driving force behind this book, and I am forever grateful for the opportunity to share these stories with you. **Because We Were In Love**, we were changed forever.

Contents

Chapter 1
Gathering In Darjeeling

The air was crisp, and the sun cast a golden glow over the picturesque hill town of Darjeeling. Five individuals, all millionaires in their own right, had gathered in this serene location with a shared purpose: to purchase a tea garden. As they stepped out of their luxurious vehicles, the atmosphere crackled with anticipation, and the scent of freshly brewed tea wafted through the air.

This is the story of five investment bankers who made a name for themselves in the industry. They had worked hard, made a lot of money, and built successful careers, but after years of doing the same thing, they had grown bored and restless. They longed for a new challenge - something that would push them outside their comfort zones and help them find new meaning in their lives.

The five millionaires came from diverse backgrounds, each with their own unique story of success. Their paths had converged in the world of business, and now, they sought to venture into the realm of tea production. Each had a vision - a dream of creating their brand of exquisite tea and leaving a lasting mark in the industry. Also, in doing so, they were able to find greater fulfillment and satisfaction in their lives. They knew each other from their professions and were connected.

After much research and discussion, they found the perfect tea garden that they could afford. It was a beautiful property with breathtaking views of the surrounding hills, a lush tea plantation, and a charming old bungalow that would be their home during the tea harvest season. Investing in tea gardens in Darjeeling can have a positive impact on the local economy by creating jobs and contributing to the community. It can also promote sustainable agriculture practices and support the local environment. This fulfills their ambition to invest the money earned in bringing change to people's lives.

They thought a lot about the venue to put their money into, and they finalized Darjeeling for its premium quality tea, constant demand, and, of course, low maintenance. They zeroed in on this as the location, and then they all decided to meet in Darjeeling to finalize the purchase and start their new venture.

As they arrived in Darjeeling, they all felt a sense of excitement and anticipation about their new business venture. They rented a large bungalow on the outskirts of Darjeeling, overlooking the rolling hills and the majestic Kanchenjunga peak. Since they knew each other professionally, they decided to introduce each other, and this time, more personally than just the professional stuff, which they all knew anyway.

The first banker, Arjun, had spent over a decade as the CEO of Arjun Inc., but he began to feel like he had accomplished all he could in the banking industry. He wanted to use his skills and knowledge to make a difference in other areas, so he decided to leave the bank and start a philanthropic foundation that would focus on education and economic development. He saw the tea garden as an opportunity to embrace nature and reconnect with his roots. Arjun envisioned a blend that married tradition and modernity, a tea that would captivate the palates of tea connoisseurs worldwide.

The second banker, Rohan, had led Goldman Sachs through a period of unprecedented success, but he had grown tired of the constant pressure and long hours. He wanted to explore his creative side and pursue his passion for art, so he retired from banking and became a full-time artist. He saw the tea garden as a chance to expand her empire and bring a touch of elegance to the world of tea. Rohan imagined packaging the tea in opulent, handcrafted boxes, creating an experience that went beyond mere consumption.

The third banker, Nikhil, had risen through the ranks at J.P. Morgan Asset Management and had become one of the most powerful men in finance. For him, the tea garden represented an investment opportunity and a chance to diversify his portfolio. He had studied the tea industry meticulously and saw the potential for exponential growth in the coming years.

Nikhil envisioned expanding the tea garden and exporting their unique blends to tea-loving nations worldwide.

The fourth banker, Ankit, had taken over as CEO of Goldman Sachs and had led the bank to new heights, but he had always been interested in music and wanted to pursue it more seriously. He left the banking industry and became a DJ, performing at clubs and festivals around the world. He saw the tea garden as a platform to champion ethical production and create a positive impact on the environment and local communities. Ankit imagined cultivating tea leaves without harmful pesticides and providing fair wages to the workers, setting an example for the industry.

The fifth banker, Rishi, had been the CEO of Barclays and had helped turn the bank around, but he had grown disillusioned with the industry and wanted to do something completely different. He left banking and started a company that focused on sustainable energy and reducing carbon emissions. He saw the tea garden as a blank canvas, an opportunity to infuse art and culture into the tea-drinking experience. Rishi envisioned hosting unique events and blending various artistic disciplines with tea tasting, creating a fusion that would appeal to the senses and spark curiosity.

As the five millionaires gathered, they exchanged introductions and shared their visions for the tea garden. Excitement filled the air as they realized the potential of their combined talents and resources. They were ready to embark on this journey together, united by their passion for tea and desire to create something extraordinary.

And so, the story of these five millionaires meeting at Darjeeling to buy a tea garden began with their dreams and aspirations intertwining to shape a new chapter in the world of tea production. Little did they know that their collaboration would lead to a remarkable blend of entrepreneurship, innovation, and a profound love for the ancient art of tea-making.

It was the first time they even started talking about personal stuff, and they started enjoying the discussion. They had all the time in the world with them, so they decided to talk about their school days, their girlfriend, or stories about how they chose to be investment bankers. So now, they have decided to begin their parts of the stories in turn. To make the stories cling to their minds, they added the flavor of the finest wines found in Darjeeling, and soon, they were completely absorbed in the tale. The night has indeed barely begun.

The sun began its descent behind the rolling hills of Darjeeling, casting a warm, golden glow over the sprawling tea garden. Amidst the vibrant greenery, a picturesque seating area had been prepared for the five millionaires. Elegant chairs adorned with plush cushions encircled a low, intricately carved wooden table. Delicate tea sets, filled with steaming cups of aromatic Darjeeling tea, awaited their arrival.

As the five millionaires approached the seating area, a sense of anticipation hung in the air. They took their seats, their eyes sparkling with excitement and curiosity.

The rhythmic chirping of birds and the gentle rustling of leaves provided a soothing soundtrack to this momentous occasion.

A gentle breeze danced through the tea leaves, carrying the fragrance of jasmine and hints of earthy undertones. The tea garden seemed to come alive as if it recognized the significance of the gathering and whispered tales of its rich history and untapped potential.

Silence settled among them, and there was a shared understanding that this was the moment they had all been waiting for. Arjun broke the silence with his distinguished demeanor, his voice resonating with a blend of confidence and humility. He spoke of his ancestors' entrepreneurial endeavors and how he longed to connect with nature and his heritage through this tea garden.

Rohan, exuding elegance and grace, joined the conversation, her voice carrying an air of authority. He spoke passionately about his vision to create a brand of tea that would redefine luxury, a tea that would elevate the sensory experience and reflect his impeccable taste.

Nikhil added his thoughts to the discussion, his eyes sharp and observant. With a touch of the Japanese tea ceremony's meticulousness, he spoke of the immense potential for growth and expansion in the tea industry, highlighting the strategic opportunities and the global market waiting to be tapped.

Embodying compassion and commitment, Ankit expressed his desire to champion sustainable and ethical practices within the tea garden. He spoke of creating a model of farming that would nurture the environment, support local communities, and provide teas of the highest quality without compromising on social responsibility.

Rishi, vibrant and vivacious, injected a sense of artistic flair into the conversation. His voice filled with passion as he shared his plans to infuse the tea garden with creativity and culture, imagining interactive events, performances, and installations that would breathe life into the tea-drinking experience.

As they shared their stories and dreams, a synergy emerged among them. The unique perspectives and experiences of each millionaire intertwined harmoniously, forming a tapestry of ambition, creativity, and expertise. They realized their individual visions were merely pieces of a grand puzzle, awaiting the final connection.

And so, as the sun dipped below the horizon, casting hues of orange and purple across the tea garden, the five millionaires found themselves united by a shared purpose. They knew that together, they possessed the power to create something truly extraordinary; a tea garden that would be more than just a business venture would be a testament to their collective passion, innovation, and dedication.

With renewed determination and a sense of camaraderie, they clinked their tea cups together, their eyes gleaming with anticipation for the journey that lay ahead. The stage was set, and their stories had converged into a symphony of possibilities - a symphony reverberating through the tea garden and beyond, leaving an indelible mark on the world of teaful.

As these tales of love intertwined with their aspirations for the tea garden, a realization dawned on the five millionaires. Love was not just a personal experience confined to their individual lives; it was a force that transcended boundaries, nurturing their ambitions and infusing their endeavors with passion, empathy, and a deeper sense of purpose.

And so, as they concluded their stories, a newfound appreciation for love's transformative power settled upon the group. They recognized that their love stories had shaped them into who they are today - individuals driven by compassion, determination, and a desire to make a positive impact on the world.

With their love stories as a guiding light, the millionaires forged ahead, not only as business partners but also as friends bonded by shared experiences of love and the belief that love, in all its forms, had the power to enrich every aspect of their lives. Rounds of wine toasting started, and the stories started becoming a bit more personal.

Arjun had been married for some time now. He talked about how he had met his wife, Anjali, in college and how they had fallen in love. Despite facing several challenges in their relationship, they remained committed to each other and grew stronger over the years.

Rohan shared his story of finding love in an unexpected place. He talked about how he had met his wife, Radhika, while on a hiking trip in the Himalayas. They had bonded over their love share for nature and adventure, and after several months of dating, they got married. He credited their shared interests and values for their strong relationship.

Nikhil talked about how he had met his wife, Sneha, at a startup conclave. He was attending this conclave as an investor. There, he met Sneha, who struck up a conversation with him. They had connected over their shared love for literature and music, and within a few months, they had started dating. They had been married for almost seven years, and he still felt lucky to have found someone who understood him so well.

Ankit shared his experience of finding love after a long time. He had been single for several years and had almost given up on finding someone. But then he met Riya at a Client's Meeting. They had bonded over their love for dancing and spent the entire night on the dance floor. After that night, they started dating and finally got married with their parents' blessing.

Rishi, who had been married for over 15 years, shared his experience of finding love in a long-term relationship. He talked about how he had met his wife, Sophia, and how they had grown together over the years. Despite facing several challenges in their relationship, they always found a way to work through them. He credited their shared sense of humor and their ability to communicate honestly.

Soon, they realized that they had a unique sense of how to explain their current relationships and also realized that they all had a past that helped them transform into what they are today. They decided to take a turn and talk about their transformation. This will also give them an opportunity to understand each other a bit better.

Chapter 2
The Fragments of Love

As the conversation flowed among the millionaires, Arjun, a member of the group, found himself compelled to share a different kind of love story. Though he was married to Anjali, his heart carried the memories of his first love, Disha.

Arjun's voice trembled slightly as he began to speak; a mix of nostalgia and vulnerability filled the air. His emotions soared like a symphony as his words revealed the tremors of that starlit night. He recounted the days of his youth when he was a carefree and adventurous soul, exploring the world with wide-eyed wonder. It was during that time that he met Disha, a captivating and free-spirited woman who had captured his heart.

With a hint of melancholy, Arjun described the moments he and Disha shared an enchanting summer romance that felt like a dream. Their love had bloomed against a backdrop of breathtaking landscapes, late-night conversations under the stars, and stolen kisses hidden from the world. Their intense and passionate connection ignited a fire within Arjun's soul. Arjun started.

"I was born and raised in a small town in India, where my parents worked hard to provide for the family. My father was a banker and was posted to the rural branch of Samastipur in Bihar. This was a small village with hardly 300 houses." Said Arjun.

As he started, memories danced within his soul with vibrant colors, a woven tapestry of moments he wished to reject, a merging of past and present intertwined, revealing a tale where heart and soul found harmony. In hesitant tones, he mustered the courage to share a delicate echo of dreams and sorrows, whispering words drifting on the breeze, conveying a story perceived only by the heart. The air carried a poignant melody, Enveloped by vulnerability's grip, a gentle rhythm, a fragile sanctuary where longing and yearning found solace in each other.

Nestled amidst the serene countryside of Samastipur district in Bihar, a charming small village called Asinpur exuded simplicity, warmth, and a close-knit community spirit. As he approached the village, the landscape transformed into a patchwork of lush green fields dotted with tall, swaying palm trees and traditional thatched-roof houses.

The village was cradled by a meandering river, its gentle flow providing a lifeline to the community. The air was imbued with the earthy scent of fertile soil and the sweet fragrance of blooming flowers that lined the village paths. The sound of chirping birds and the distant lowing of cows further enriched the serene ambiance.

Agriculture formed the backbone of the village's economy. Fields stretched as far as the eye can see, cultivated with crops such as rice, wheat, and pulses. Villagers, dressed in vibrant traditional attire, could be seen working in the fields, tending to the crops with care and dedication. The agricultural cycle dictated the rhythm of life here, with festivals and rituals closely tied to the changing seasons and harvests.

Education held great importance in the village as a symbol of progress and empowerment. A modest school stands proudly, nurturing young minds and providing them with the knowledge to shape their future. The sound of children's laughter and the echo of their eager voices filled the classrooms, reflecting the village's aspirations for a brighter tomorrow. The good school was around 30 kilometers from the village. This was where kids from such government institutions study when they are transferred.

I was in 10th grade. This was a really difficult period for a student. The pressure of studies was already there, and a transfer to a new town and a new school was the icing on the cake. There's no time to make friends or for anything else after school because I needed to focus on my studies and get good marks. Although I was good at my studies, I was still worried.

Traveling to school every day was the most tedious part of my day. I used to sit in the corner seat of the bus. It was a passenger bus, not a dedicated school bus.

Getting a seat was the biggest hassle every day. Bihar, anyhow, was not known for having a lot of schools with school buses in those days. Arjun smiled and added.

"This seat you are sitting on is for ladies. You need to get up from here." Someone from the back told me.

I was annoyed as soon as I heard this. I turned back to see who said this. My attention was captivated by a girl dressed in the familiar school uniform standing there, blowing bubbles with her gum, exuding an air of carefree charm.

The way she blew those bubbles, with her eyes twinkling with mischief and a playful smile dancing on her lips, created an enchanting aura around her. The rhythmic pop of the bubbles seemed to synchronize with the beating of your heart as an unspoken connection began to form. I was immediately drawn to her beauty and grace.

All of a sudden, I realized that the noise around the bus was gone. I just felt like I was alone on the bus with some nice music playing in the background. The light had gone dim around me, and there were just two of us around. The music started getting more and more prominent, and I started getting deeper and deeper into it. I didn't even realize the surroundings I was in at that time.

"Hello, are you dumb?" shouted one of her friends, and they started laughing together.

I suddenly realized that this was for me. "Sorry," I said, moving out of the seat. One of her friends sat like a queen in the seat, and the rest stood. As I moved out, they all laughed again. I went back and stood in a corner, occasionally lifting my head to see the beautiful red lips and the bubble gum coming out of them. I was lost in the dream and blushed the whole journey. The same music, the same dim light within the bus, and I stood straight, looking at her.

As I was lost in my dreams and red lips, the ticket collector on the bus shook me to tell me that we had reached the school. I realized that today we reached the school much sooner than before. Everyone got off the bus. The gang of girls also got off, and I realized that we were all walking toward the same school gate. I was on cloud eleven when I realized that we studied at the same school. I was jumping with joy.

I was eager to find out which class she entered, and I waited at the gate to see this. It felt to me that I was on a mission to know her, talk to her, and be friends with her. With this thought going through my head, I started walking behind her. Again, I was surprised to see that she was in the same grade as I was. She was just in another section. "Yes!" I shouted as I won the Oscars and went to my class happily. The day just started, and I was already eager for it to end. I was eager to be on the same bus while going back and discover her home address, too.

The day passed somehow, and it was time to go back home. My eagerness turned into curiosity. I had a strange feeling of butterflies in my stomach. I was feeling nervous and excited when I was around her. I wanted to know more about her. I wanted to spend more and more time with her, but I was not sure how to do this. It was not very easy for me, as being new to the town, I still didn't have many friends. I was also not very open with everyone and had no friends with whom to express myself. Overall, this was a roller coaster of emotions for me.

"So, have you gathered the courage to talk to her that evening?" "What was her reaction?" Nikhil inquired, as he sounded interested.

"Patience," said Arjun. "It was not very easy for me to express myself. I was introverted by nature, and I also had strict parents. They didn't want me to be distracted from my studies. They wanted me to get good marks, opt for science, and move to Kota to prepare for the IIT entrance exam. Although I was good at studying, I still didn't want to be part of this race. I wanted to be a musician. I used to play guitar, and I was good at singing. I wanted to pursue that as a career, and in my secret world, I already see myself as a famous and successful singer."

"Coming back to my story," said Arjun, taking a sip of wine. "That evening, I followed her to her home, where I discovered that she stayed near my colony. She was the daughter of the owner of a famous "Agarwal sweets" in our village, and they were decently affluent. She also used to be in the shop in the evenings, helping out her parents. Now, I knew where to see her frequently.

The very next day, I asked my parents for some money and went to her shop to buy some sweets. In fact, I wanted to see her and know her name. Sweet was just an excuse to visit the shop. I was lucky to have her at the counter that day. I went to her and started asking about various sweets in a shivering voice. As soon as she saw me, she started laughing, which confused me. I ran away from the shop without buying anything. She continued laughing. I never gathered the courage to visit the shop again out of shame over my first performance. Teenagers are too crazy sometimes and make life complicated by overthinking some of these aspects. We only understand this once we are grown up and have passed that stage. Looking for her on the bus and seeing her in school from afar has become my daily ritual. I was doing this very secretively without her knowing about it. This went on for months, and those were the most exciting days of my life until today.

This was my third month in the school, and we had our school's annual day coming up. Many programs were getting listed for this day, and I too had a solo performance lined up for me. I got busy with my practice. As previously said, I loved to sing and play the guitar and spent countless hours practicing and honing my skills. Although my parents wanted me to be good at my studies, they were fine with me spending some time with music, and they used to be supportive of my skill. They were happy that they received a special invitation to the function as I was performing. I got a bit busy with that and also started missing my daily ritual of seeing her. Fast forward to the day of the annual function, and I performed well. I received great applause from the audience, and the event was a success from my point of view. I tried seeing her from the stage, but I didn't find her.

The next day, on our bus, she came and sat next to me. I was lucky that day that the seat was empty. She also didn't have her gang of girls around her. This was unusual, but as there is a saying, when it's your day, everything falls into place. "You sing very well," she said. I said thank you. "You play guitar also very well," she said again. "Thank you," I again replied. She took her hand forward and said, "My name is Disha, and yours." "Arjun," I said, shaking hands with her. "Friends," she said, and I shook my head "yes". She smiled, and seeing her smiling face this close to me made me happy. For once, I felt that her smile was not mischievous but warm and inviting. I smiled back at her. She then asked about how good I am at mathematics and offered to do some sort of combined study and prepare together for the exams.

She was not that bad at studying but wanted some company. I was really glad that she made this offer. We chose the school library to spend time together, solving some complex mathematical equations. I was excited and always looked forward to having sessions with Disha in the library. Although this was not very helpful for me in terms of improving my grade, as my focus was entirely on her, I was still very involved and was looking forward to the afternoon sessions in the library. After all, that was the only chance for me to stay close to her. Sometimes, I was close enough to smell the fragrance of perfume she used to wear, and that used to take me to a different world altogether.

What a day and what a feeling! I have never experienced that feeling so far, I must confess."

Rohan interrupted in between and asked, "What happened to your love?" You started telling us the story of mathematics, but we are more interested in your love story than mathematical equations. Have you proposed to her? Has something happened between you two? Please tell us more. Don't stop. The story is very interesting.

Rohan, my brother, I was an introvert, and it's not very easy to get someone like me to express myself, and I never dared to move beyond the mathematical equations. Sometimes, during the sessions, her hand accidentally touched mine, and that was what I would consider the maximum that can happen between us. I still remember her first touch. Her touch was used to convey a wide range of emotions and feelings. When she touched me for the first time, it evoked a variety of sensations and emotions, and the feeling is really difficult for me to explain in words. Just understand that I used to feel as if someone had let the whole electricity flow through my body, and I am enjoying that rather than dying. That moment of confusion between dying and enjoyment is the moment I always wanted to be in, and the sweet fragrance coming from her was enough for me to feel motivated to come back to the library the next day. That was the moment I used to live for, and I wouldn't have complained to the Almighty at all if that could have been the last moment of my life. What a feeling that was.

"Wow," said Rishi. "You took me to my teens, and I am experiencing all these things happening in front of me. I am eager to understand what happened next. How was your first kiss, and who initiated it? Go ahead and jump directly to this, please. I am eager."

"Shut up, Rishi," said Nikhil. "I am enjoying the pace at which it's flowing." "Let it flow, and Arjun, don't stop in between, please."

"I was too naive to think about kissing at that time. It was more of a love where I just wanted to be with her, see her, spend time with her, and keep hearing her talk rather than kiss and send other physical signals, which couples usually do to show love. I am not saying that it's wrong, but I didn't have that as my intention," said Arjun.

With every word he spoke, a new part of the story emerged. His voice carried emotions gently wrapped within, like a comforting hug; memories from the past echoed, creating a personal picture never witnessed before. The melody of nostalgia played on invisible strings, a heartfelt song of remembrance, and a deeply rooted routine. His voice became a vessel for hidden feelings, revealing the profound depths of a captivating tale. Arjun's voice danced like a mystical waltz through time, resonating with echoes of his inner self. As the stars shimmered, ready to divulge their secrets, his trembling voice uncovered a world so exceptionally rare. He continued.

"Time flew by, and we started seeing each other more and more on the bus, in school, in the library, in her shop, and almost everywhere. This started taking a toll on my studies. I was busy thinking about her and the ways to keep seeing her, and in doing all this, I forgot that we would have to face the board exam very soon. There came January, and I was not even done with my syllabus. It didn't take me ages to realize that I was not doing well in my academics and I needed to bring my focus back. My parents were not very happy to see my grades coming down.

I shared my parents' wish with Disha about moving to Kota to focus on the IIT entrance exam. She had also convinced her parents about the same. We were happy that we would get to spend time together in an unknown city far from where they were currently. The best thing about that was that we would have plenty of time to spend together. We were both happy, and we both worked together towards this goal.

Lately, a growing concern had taken hold of me, gradually intensifying as I found myself struggling in my academic pursuits. The weight of this worry had settled upon my shoulders, casting a shadow over my thoughts and daily endeavors. The realization that I was not performing as well as I desired in my studies had begun to gnaw at the corners of my mind, stirring restlessness and unease within me. Each passing day brought a heightened sense of anxiety as I grappled with the implications of my academic shortcomings and the potential consequences they may entail. The fear of falling behind, not meeting expectations, and the uncertainty of what lies ahead had become constant companions, lingering like an unwelcome cloud overhead. This worry infiltrated my thoughts, leaving me with a lingering sense of unease, a persistent reminder of the need to address and overcome the challenges I faced in my educational journey.

As the exams approached, I began to feel increasingly anxious and stressed. I knew that I had not prepared well and felt overwhelmed by the thought of failing. This fear of failing or not doing well in exams overshadows all the confidence I have built all these days. I started being worried and had also stopped seeing Disha until the exams were over. I had told Disha about this already, so she was not worried. It was increasingly difficult for me to focus on preparations, and the matter started slipping from my hands. I did all I could in a short period of time to correct the situation, but it didn't take me long to realize that I was in big trouble.

Thoughts of not doing well in exams were making it even more difficult to accept this. I started getting worried about what my parents would say and how I would deal with the situation. What would happen to our Kota plan, and what would happen if Disha was the only one to be in Kota alone? A lot of questions and no answers were making me sick.

On the day of the exams, I felt sick with nerves. I had a knot in my stomach and couldn't concentrate on the questions in front of me. I struggled to recall the information I had learned and couldn't complete the paper within the allotted time. I was so tense and worried after the exam that I didn't stop to catch up with Disha. I rushed home so that I could prepare for the next exam. This was my routine for almost all the exams. I was worried that I hadn't performed as well as I wanted to.

Now, the exams were over, and I knew that I had messed up with the exams, and I could see my dreams get shattered. Now, I was just praying to get enough marks to be able to get through any of the coaching institutions in Kota rather than the best ones. I met Disha a few times in the meantime and checked on her exams. She was very confident that the combined studies done in the library were going to help her a lot. She was confident even though she was not among the toppers in the school. This made me even more worried, and I started lying to her about my exam. We kept meeting and planning our Kota days.

Somewhere deep inside, I already knew that I had lost this. I started getting prepared mentally for the worst to come. Although it was not easy for me to even imagine it, I was kind of trying to come out of it. I felt a deep sense of sadness and despair, which led me to withdraw from others and become socially isolated. I felt like I had lost a part of myself and had a great struggle imagining a future without their love. I experienced anger and resentment, and a feeling that I could have focused a bit more on my studies and that things could have been a bit better than this today.

The day came when the results were declared. I was excited to discover my result and also how my plans with Disha were going to work out. I met Disha at the bus stand, and we rushed towards the school to get the result. It was the good old days when the results were posted on the notice board of the school rather than on the internet. Other curious students and parents were waiting eagerly at the school for the results. My father had an urgent meeting at the bank, so he asked me to come and update him at the bank as soon as the result was out. Disha was excited about the result and jumping in joy, thinking about how good her exams were.

The bell rang, and we all rushed to the notice board. I was really slow to move toward the notice board, but Disha dragged me there. Disha jumped with joy as soon as she saw her marks. She deserved to jump for joy, as she was the school topper for the year. She looked at me with joy and shouted, "Yes, I have done it." Now, I, too, started searching for my name. I skipped the top 20-25 names and started from there, hoping my name would be somewhere in the middle of the class of 60 students in my section. I finally found my name somewhere around the 55th or 56th row. When I looked at the percentage, it was around 49%. My heart sank, and I walked toward Disha to tell her my marks.

"Hey, we are going to Kota." My parents will be more than happy to send me to Kota with the grades I have gotten. "All our plans will materialize now, and I am happy," shouted Disha joyfully.

I interrupted her and told her my marks. She was surprised to discover this. All of a sudden, her excitement went away, and she started getting pale. She was in a state of shock for a while. I, too, was standing there without any sense of my surroundings. I was feeling as if I had gone dumb all of a sudden, and I could hear nobody. I can sense that even Disha was in the same state.

"What will happen to us now? My parents have heard a lot about Kota and IIT from me. They have already made all the arrangements for me to go, and I am sure I cannot step back now. I would definitely have to go. What will happen to us now? Would you still be able to make it to Kota with these grades?" Disha started blabbering out of confusion.

I told her that with these grades, none of the coaching would even entertain me; forget about Kota and IIT. My parents would also be unhappy with this, and I would have no further courage to talk about moving out of the house for a school anywhere else.

"Why don't you tell your parents that you no longer want to go to IIT and tell them that your interest changed?" I further suggested it to Disha.

"Are you kidding, Arjun?" said Disha. "How can you say this now?" "I worked hard because it was our dream, and now you are asking me to leave something for which I have worked really hard." She has started growing impatient now.

"I wasted a lot of time around you, and that's why this is the result. I could have been a bit more aware before and avoided seeing this day." Overwhelmed by a turbulent whirlwind of emotions, I found myself caught in a disorienting state of confusion, and in that moment of chaos, I impulsively raised my voice towards her. The weight of my inner turmoil had clouded my judgment, obscuring my ability to respond with clarity and understanding. Frustration and a sense of being overwhelmed by the circumstances enveloped me, fueling the impulsive outburst that escaped my lips. Regret and remorse swiftly followed as the realization of my actions sunk in. The echoes of my raised voice reverberated through the air, filled with a mix of anger, confusion, and the desperate need to make sense of the tumultuous thoughts that plagued my mind. I felt a pang of guilt for allowing my inner turmoil to manifest in such an unkind manner, fully aware that my words carried the power to wound and leave lasting scars. In that moment of confusion, I yearned for clarity, for a sense of calm that could unravel the knots of my tangled emotions.

"You are blaming me for this, Arjun. I never asked you to come behind me. In fact, I never asked you for anything. I just followed what we planned, or, in fact, what you have planned for us. You are a loser, and I am going away." Said Disha in anger and moved away from there. I stood there looking at her with mixed emotions, wanting to stop her but not stop her. I felt cheated at that moment.

A profound sense of unease began to settle within me as a disheartening realization took hold. I had come to believe that Disha, whom I had trusted and cared for, had been manipulating and taking advantage of my presence in her life. Over time, a series of puzzling events and subtle cues had gradually woven together, forming a tapestry of doubt and suspicion. The warmth and sincerity that once characterized our interactions now seemed tainted, as if every exchange had been carefully orchestrated to serve her hidden agenda. The weight of this revelation grew heavier with each passing day as I retraced our shared moments, questioning their authenticity and sincerity.

The once vibrant colors of our bond now appeared faded, shrouded in a cloud of disillusionment. Waves of hurt and betrayal crashed against the shores of my heart, leaving behind fragments of broken trust and a profound sense of being used. The impact of this realization weighed heavily upon my thoughts, casting shadows of doubt over all my past interactions, leaving me to grapple with a complex mix of emotions - from anger and resentment to sadness and a deep longing for answers. I found myself caught in a whirlwind of introspection, desperately seeking clarity and closure while grappling with the lingering ache of being deceived and used.

I felt that Disha had used me all these days to get good grades and had never really cared about me as a friend. I was angry and frustrated, and I blamed Disha for my failure. In fact, I was analyzing my entire year to understand what I had done and how I had avoided my goal to find myself in this state today. I was equally worried about the reactions of my parents. There were heaps of confusion in my head, and I was not thinking about anything other than myself.

After all that, I reached the bank to let my father know the result. My father was excited to see me at the bank because he wanted to know the result. He became furious as soon as I told him about the result. Unfortunately, it happens to some parents. They start reacting negatively to their child's academic performance. They may criticize their child, belittle their efforts, or even punish them for not achieving their goals. This kind of response can damage to a child's self-esteem and motivation. But I took all these standing in front of my father in the bank, in front of all the colleagues. I just ran away from the bank when I reached my limits, went home, and locked myself in my room for the full day.

As the truth unraveled before my eyes, my heart was gripped by an overwhelming sorrow that seemed to fracture and splinter its very core. The news of Disha's decision to embark on a journey to Kota without extending an invitation for me to accompany her pierced through my soul like a thousand shards of glass. In that instant, the world around me seemed to crumble, and my spirit plummeted into a depth of heartbreak and desolation.

Every beat of my shattered heart echoed with a profound sense of loss and abandonment. Waves of anguish washed over me, leaving me gasping for air amidst the ruins of our once-shared dreams and aspirations. The dreams we had woven together, the plans and promises we made, now lay in ruins like a broken mosaic, mocking the fragility of our bond.

A profound sense of emptiness settled within me as I grappled with the cruel reality of her departure without me. Questions whirled in my mind, tormenting me with their unanswerable nature. Why was I left behind? What had caused this sudden rupture in our connection? The ache of longing and the void of her absence seemed unbearable as the weight of her departure bore down upon my shoulders.

Each step she would take towards Kota felt like a jagged knife twisting deeper into my wounded heart. The images of her moving forward without me, forging ahead on a path we had once envisioned together, intensified the anguish within. It was as if the very fabric of our shared hopes and aspirations had been violently torn apart, leaving behind jagged edges of unfulfilled dreams and shattered promises.

In the wake of this heart-wrenching revelation, I found myself grappling with a myriad of emotions. Grief, betrayal, and an overwhelming sense of abandonment intertwined, leaving me lost in a labyrinth of pain and confusion. The realization that our paths had diverged, and that I had been left behind shattered the foundation of trust I had so willingly placed in our bond.

In the aftermath of this devastating discovery, I stood on the precipice of healing and rebuilding, my broken heart still tender and raw. The journey ahead seemed daunting, but I knew that with time and self-care, I would gather the shattered fragments of my heart and find solace in mending my wounded spirit.

"I can't believe you decided to leave without me," I said, my voice dripping with anger. "You never even thought once about us before taking this decision."

"It was our dream, Arjun," Disha replied, her voice shaking. "Just because you changed the goalposts in between and started neglecting your studies, I cannot be blamed for that now."

"I didn't change the goalpost." "It was just your presence that I was not able to focus on anything else," Arjun shot back. "Now, you were only thinking about yourself and your own ambitions."

"That's not true, Arjun," Disha said, tears streaming down her face. "I care about you and your dreams. But I can't let your anger and bitterness hold me back."

Arjun scoffed. "Typical. You always put yourself first, Disha, and you don't care about anyone else's feelings."

A deep-seated concern gripped me as I grappled with the unsettling realization that Disha, in her actions and choices consistently prioritized her own needs and desires above the feelings and well-being of others. It was as if a veil had been lifted, revealing a pattern of self-centeredness that had previously gone unnoticed. The weight of this revelation settled upon my heart, causing it to ache with a sense of disappointment and hurt.

The argument escalated from there, with both of us saying hurtful things to each other. In the end, I stormed out of the room, slamming the door behind her. Disha was alone, sobbing, and heartbroken.

Every encounter and every interaction seemed to underscore this self-centric approach. I couldn't help but feel a sense of frustration and disillusionment as it became increasingly evident that Disha's choices were driven by personal gain, regardless of the impact on those around her. The empathy and consideration that I had hoped for seemed to be overshadowed by her own ambitions and self-interest.

The absence of genuine concern for others left me with a lingering sense of emotional neglect. It felt as though my own feelings, as well as those of others, were inconsequential in the face of her self-focused perspective. The realization that my emotions and needs were disregarded in favor of her own left me feeling invisible and unimportant.

The aftermath of our breakup reverberated with an indescribable pain, enveloping both of us in the depths of sorrow and heartache. The realization that our journey had come to an abrupt end after an entire year of shared experiences, cherished memories, and intertwined dreams shattered our spirits.

The fragments of what was once a vibrant and promising relationship lay scattered in the echoes of our separation. Each broken shard held within it a reminder of the love and connection we had nurtured, now severed and rendered into painful remnants. The weight of loss and the void left in its wake felt insurmountable as we grappled with the absence of a future we had once envisioned together.

The memories we had woven throughout that year now felt bittersweet, as the joy and happiness they once brought were now tinged with a profound sense of loss. The laughter and shared moments that once formed the fabric of our togetherness now served as poignant reminders of what we had lost. Once intertwined and fueled by mutual passion, our dreams now lay in ruins, leaving us adrift in a sea of uncertainty.

Grief permeated every aspect of our lives, casting shadows over the places we had been, the experiences we had shared, and the dreams we had dared to dream. The pain of separation reverberated within our hearts, leaving an indelible mark on our souls. It was as if a part of us had been wrenched away, leaving an emptiness that seemed impossible to fill.

Navigating the shattered remains of our relationship required us to confront the stark reality of moving forward separately. The once-familiar path we had walked together had diverged, leaving us to face the unknown alone. The journey of healing and rebuilding stretched before us, demanding resilience and courage as we sought to piece together our lives and find solace amidst the ruins.

In the aftermath of our painful breakup, we clung to the memories and the lessons learned, even as we struggled to let go. Each shattered piece of our past held significance, a testament to the love and growth we had experienced. While the pain was overwhelming, we were left with a glimmer of hope that, in time, we would heal, grow, and forge new paths that would eventually lead us to find happiness once again.

I struggled to come to terms with the end of their relationship. I missed Disha terribly, but I was still angry and bitter about the way things had turned out. Amidst the turmoil, I found myself grappling with conflicting emotions, torn between the desire to hold onto what we had and the need to release the toxicity that had poisoned our connection. The anger served as a defense mechanism, shielding me from the raw vulnerability of accepting the finality of our relationship. It provided a temporary refuge, a shield against the pain that threatened to consume me entirely.

As I journeyed through the labyrinth of emotions, I sought solace in introspection and self-reflection. I recognized the importance of acknowledging and processing these difficult emotions, understanding that healing and growth would require confronting the bitterness and anger that had taken root within me. It became clear that finding closure would necessitate letting go of the resentment that bound me, granting myself the freedom to heal and move forward.

In the midst of missing Disha terribly, I strived to find a delicate balance between honoring the love we once shared and allowing myself to release the toxic emotions that hindered my own wellbeing. It was a challenging path, one that required patience, self-compassion, and the willingness to embark on a journey of forgiveness and self-discovery.

I tried to distract myself by focusing on music, but the pain of losing Disha was always there. I am sure it was not easy for Disha either, but by now we had already stopped seeing each other, and then I discovered that she had already moved to Kota.

After this, I threw myself into studies and music, trying to forget and get past Disha. I got to select commerce as my subject at the same school. Although my parents were not very happy about it, I decided to forget my past and make this big. I always had Disha in my memories. Later, I realized that it was my mistake and that I could not have reacted this badly. I always wanted to go back to her and apologize for my behavior, but time never gave me a chance to do so.

I did my bachelor's in commerce and then an MBA from IIM, Ahmedabad. This is where I met Anjali and this time I knew that I don't have to do the same mistakes I already did. There were ups and downs in the relationship, but we sailed through. I started working as a banker in a private bank and eventually grew into an investment banker myself. Together, we are happy but somewhere deep, I still want the time to be revived so that I get a chance to apologize for my act to Disha. I am sure I will never have the courage to go back to her however successful I will be.

The haunting presence of the last tears that welled up in my eyes lingers within me, an enduring reminder of a profound emotional pain. The weight of guilt, heavy and relentless, burdens my heart as I grapple with the persistent notion that I failed to muster the courage to claim my own failures as my personal responsibility.

Those tears, cascading down my cheeks, bore witness to the depths of my inner turmoil. They held within them a torrent of emotions, a poignant reflection of my own vulnerability and the fear that consumed me. Each drop, a testament to my struggle to confront the reality of my shortcomings, became etched into my memory, an indelible mark of my perceived inadequacy.

Guilt, like a relentless specter, follows me wherever I go. Its presence seeps into every corner of my consciousness, a constant reminder of the perceived missed opportunities and the hesitation that held me captive. I am haunted by the relentless question of what could have been, the unrelenting self-reproach for not having the strength to confront and accept my failures with unwavering boldness.

The burden of not claiming my failures as my own weighs heavily upon me, casting shadows over my self-esteem and casting doubt upon my worthiness. It is a continuous struggle to find redemption from this guilt, as I question my own abilities and the decisions that led me to this point. I yearn for a release from the shackles of this remorse, longing to break free from the grip of self-blame and embrace the opportunity for growth and self-forgiveness.

The echoes of that guilt reverberate through my thoughts, reminding me of the lessons learned and the potential for personal transformation. It is a delicate dance between acknowledging the pain of my perceived shortcomings and granting myself the grace to heal. The journey toward self-acceptance and the liberation from this guilt is an arduous one, but I hold onto the glimmer of hope that lies within, knowing that true healing begins with compassion, understanding, and the courage to face my own vulnerabilities.

"A compact, yet profound love story etches itself onto the canvas of life, leaving an indelible mark upon the heart. Though brief in duration, its impact resonates with a power that defies time and space. It is a tale that encapsulates the intensity and transformative nature of love, forever shaping the trajectory of our existence." Ankit said, tossing his glass and thinking deeply.

Yes. Its impact is far-reaching, forever altering the course of those who partake in its tender embrace. The memories forged within this concise love story become cherished fragments of the self, woven into the very fabric of one's being. They serve as a constant reminder of the heights and depths that love can reach, forever transforming the lens through which life is perceived.

The significance of this condensed love story lies not in its length, but in its ability to leave an everlasting imprint upon the human spirit. It serves as a testament to the capacity of love to transcend time and defy conventional expectations. Like a cherished gem, it sparkles brightly, radiating its brilliance and casting a luminous glow upon the journey of life.

"I too have something similar with my story, but it was more of a struggle to find the balance between money and love," said Rohan. "I was not rich enough to win my love forever."

"That sounds interesting," Arjun said, "why don't you go next?" Rohan started.

Chapter 3
Money Versus Love

Rohan's mind becomes a gateway to a flood of thoughts, feelings, and sensations. It becomes a doorway to the past, unlocking a tapestry of memories intricately woven within the fabric of one's consciousness.

As the mind traverses the pathways of remembrance, it reconstructs fragments of the past. Emotions, both vivid and poignant, surge forth, intensifying the experience. The mind becomes a canvas upon which these emotions are painted, each stroke capturing the essence of the story being relived. He started.

In the summer of 2003, a pivotal chapter in my life unfolded as I received acceptance into an engineering college nestled in a remote corner of Odisha. Being a proud native of Odisha, I nurtured a deep-rooted attachment to my home state and harbored a desire to pursue my studies within its borders. Despite my academic prowess falling short of securing admission to esteemed regional institutions, I embraced the opportunity that lay before me. It led me to a quaint, picturesque location nestled amidst the hills of Rayagada, a lesser - known gem within the sprawling landscape of the Koraput district.

Rayagada, a serene and enchanting town nestled within the undulating hills of the Koraput district, held a captivating allure that cast its spell upon me. As I embarked on my educational journey in this picturesque locale, I found myself captivated by its distinct charm and idyllic surroundings.

The town of Rayagada exuded a sense of tranquility, with its lush green landscapes, gently rolling hills, and soothing ambiance that seemed to embrace all who ventured within its borders. The crisp mountain air filled my lungs, invigorating my spirit and inspiring a profound connection to the natural beauty that enveloped the region.

The people, warm - hearted and welcoming, embraced me as one of their own. Their genuine hospitality and inclusive nature fostered a sense of belonging and community. Engaging in conversations with the locals, I discovered their remarkable tales, deep-rooted traditions, and profound love for their homeland.

In search of a college that would align with my aspirations, I discovered an institution that not only boasted reasonable tuition fees but also resonated with my desire for financial independence. Though I hail from a family of comfortable means, I felt reluctant to burden my parents with financial requests. Moreover, the cost of living in smaller locales proved to be notably affordable, prompting my decision to relocate.

While engineering held limited appeal for me personally, I succumbed to the prevailing trend of pursuing an engineering degree following a successful science - focused high school education in India. This remote and serene location appeared ideal for immersing myself in a transformative four-year journey, a period during which I hoped to unearth my true purpose in life.

It was not a very old college, and we had a lot of management quota seats in the college. Students from Bengal, Bihar, and Andhra Pradesh usually preferred these seats, and the college was filled with students from these states along with the locals. On the whole, it was a mixed culture in college, where you could see some sweet faces from other states too. It was also a great opportunity to learn about other states. You hardly get such chances in school.

As an eager participant in the transition from high school to college, I was filled with anticipation and enthusiasm as I embarked upon this new chapter of my life. Alongside the myriad academic and personal prospects that lay ahead, I found myself captivated by the prospect of forming romantic connections. Adhering to the prevalent social norm, I embraced the desire to seek companionship, recognizing the common occurrence of this trend among fellow students. Embracing this collective experience, I sought to forge meaningful relationships, eager to partake in the shared journey of exploration and personal growth.

On the very first day of college, it was this one girl who caught my attention. She stood out from the crowd at college. She had a sweet smile on her face, which makes it difficult to ignore her if you see her once. She had the eyes of a child, and her short hair made it so pleasant to look at her that I kept looking at her for a while until I realized it wasn't a good idea to start this on day one of college. I was happy to discover that she was also a freshman in college like me, and I was excited about the opportunity to spend at least four years with her. She also happened to get a momentary glance at me and then move on.

The curriculum of my first year in college seemed to traverse familiar territories, as the subjects mirrored the syllabus I had encountered during my high school days. Consequently, staying on track with my studies did not prove overly challenging, allowing me a significant amount of free time to explore other aspects of my college experience. It was during this time that I stumbled upon an intriguing insight shared by my seniors. The notion that a genuine engineer tended to dedicate themselves to intense studying only when faced with imminent deadlines, thus affording them the liberty to indulge in various pursuits throughout the remainder of the semester. This revelation provided an encouraging affirmation that aligned seamlessly with my own approach to academia.

As I embraced my new life in this unfamiliar town, a captivating journey of connection and companionship unfolded before me. The halls of the college and the streets of the town became fertile ground for forging new friendships, intertwining the threads of my existence with those of my fellow students and the townsfolk alike. Among the many friendly faces that graced my days, there was one whose presence brought an undeniable radiance to my world.

From the very first day of college, I encountered her, and in her smile, I found an enchanting allure that captivated my heart. Time and again, I would catch glimpses of her delightful countenance, and with each sighting, an inexplicable desire to be in her presence grew stronger. The remarkable thing was that, seemingly by chance, she appeared in various locales I frequented. Whether it was the bustling shopping area, the dimly lit movie theater, the tranquil park, or even during my morning jogs, her presence seemed to permeate every aspect of my surroundings. It was a phenomenon that both intrigued and puzzled me-a series of coincidences or perhaps a subtle hint from fate itself.

Though unaware of the true nature of these occurrences, I found immense joy in the moments I shared with her, cherishing every encounter as if it were a precious gift. Stepping out of my comfort zone, I realized that a single glimpse of her became the motivation behind my ventures into the outside world. Astonishingly, it seemed as though fortune was on my side, as these encounters became a regular part of my routine, filling my days with a sense of wonder and anticipation.

I began to question whether this unanticipated convergence was a mere coincidence or a testament to a greater cosmic design. Was it possible that our paths were destined to intersect, or was it merely the ebb and flow of chance guiding our encounters? Such ponderings only deepened the enigma surrounding our connection, leaving me in a state of awe and curiosity.

Regardless of the underlying truth, I reveled in the magic of these moments, savoring the thrill of each serendipitous meeting. The world seemed to align in mysterious ways, granting me the privilege of witnessing her presence wherever I ventured. It was an experience that transcended the ordinary, enveloping my heart in a tapestry of possibility and hope.

The question of destiny or coincidence lingered, teasing my thoughts and awakening a sense of wonder. Yet, in the midst of this uncertainty, I embraced the beauty of the journey, relishing every instance where our paths intertwined. Whether guided by fate or by chance, these encounters wove a captivating tale that I eagerly embraced, eagerly anticipating the next chapter yet to unfold.

Enshrouded in a labyrinth of desire and trepidation, I yearned for a connection with her, yet the fear of venturing into uncharted territory held me back. As a carefree and lighthearted individual, I harbored an aversion to unnecessary complications and hesitated to disrupt the tranquility that surrounded us. Thus, I maintained a cautious distance, all the while nurturing an unspoken desire for our paths to intertwine in meaningful conversation.

Within the depths of my being, a battle raged between the longing for connection and the hesitance born from a desire to avoid unnecessary conflict. It was as if a delicate dance played out within my heart, a dance of hope and apprehension, intertwining their steps in a harmonious yet cautious rhythm. I yearned for the moments where our words would meet, our thoughts would collide, and a profound understanding would be forged between us.

Yet, I remained hesitant, allowing my reservations to act as a self-imposed barrier. I feared disrupting the equilibrium and the comfortable rapport we seemed to share from afar. It was a delicate balance where my desire to bridge the divide between us warred with my aversion to inviting complications that could potentially mar our connection.

In the depths of my soul, I held a silent wish for serendipity to intervene, for the winds of fate to guide us towards the opportune moment for our paths to converge. I yearned for a connection that would transcend the boundaries of distance and hesitation, a connection grounded in genuine understanding and mutual respect.

While maintaining a safe distance, I nurtured an unspoken hope that the threads of destiny would weave together, bringing us closer in a way that felt effortless and natural. The longing to connect and converse danced alongside my desire to preserve the harmonious rhythm of our unspoken connection.

In this intricate dance of conflicting emotions, I found solace in the delicate balance, cherishing the anticipation that each passing day brought. I held onto the belief that when the time was right, our paths would converge, and the words we longed to share would flow freely, unburdened by the weight of hesitation. Until then, I embraced the enigmatic beauty of our unspoken connection, relishing the moments of serendipity and allowing the bonds between us to blossom at their own pace.

As I stood amidst the vibrant displays of a cloth shop, a symphony of colors and textures captivating my senses, the air was suddenly punctuated by a voice that resonated with familiarity. "You study at the same engineering college as me." The words echoed in my ears, accompanied by a rush of astonishment and curiosity.

Intrigued, I turned towards the source of the voice, my eyes widening in surprise as I beheld the very person who had captured my attention from afar. It was her-the same enchanting girl who had unknowingly woven herself into the fabric of my thoughts and desires. Our paths had converged in this seemingly ordinary moment, infusing it with extraordinary significance.

A whirlwind of emotions stirred within me as I exchanged glances with her, my heart racing with a mixture of excitement and anticipation. It was as if the universe had conspired to bring us together, orchestrating this chance encounter amidst the vibrant array of fabrics and threads.

In that fleeting moment, time seemed to stand still as we stood face-to-face, our connection forged by the shared space of our engineering college. The realization that we were both walking parallel paths on this educational journey ignited a spark of connection, leaving me in awe of the synchronicity that had led us to this point.

As our eyes met, a silent understanding seemed to pass between us, bridging the gap that had separated us until now. The conversation that unfolded held the promise of new beginnings and endless possibilities. It was a serendipitous moment, etching itself into the tapestry of our lives and forever intertwining our stories in a mesmerizing dance of fate and chance.

In that cloth shop, amidst bolts of fabric and the hum of everyday life, our encounter served as a testament to the unpredictable nature of destiny. It was a vivid reminder that even in the most unexpected of places, two souls can converge, setting the stage for a journey that would transcend the boundaries of coincidence and weave a tale of connection and shared experiences.

"Yes, I do," I said. "My name is Rohan, and yours?" I continued.

"I am Sonam." "I came from Delhi," she said.

With a mix of curiosity and excitement, I couldn't help but utter the question that hung in the air, "How come you are here?" It was a simple inquiry, yet it sparked the beginning of a profound conversation that would forever shape our connection.

As the words escaped my lips, an exchange unfolded, and revealing snippets of our respective stories. We embarked on a journey of discovery, gradually unraveling the layers that hid our true selves. Step by step, we ventured into the realm of shared experiences and common ground, traversing the space between strangers and newfound acquaintances.

As our conversation blossomed, we found ourselves strolling towards her hostel, our words floating effortlessly in the air, creating a bridge of understanding. The discourse flowed freely, weaving together tales of disappointment and disillusionment. She confided in me, expressing her discontent with the place that had promised so much but failed to deliver. The college management's lofty promises and exaggerated claims left her feeling trapped in an environment she couldn't fully embrace.

She lamented the lack of genuine connections, sharing her struggle to form meaningful friendships amidst the unfamiliar surroundings. It was in that vulnerable moment that I extended a gesture of companionship, offering her the warmth of my friendship. Our exchange of phone numbers became the symbolic link that bound us together, fostering a bond that would soon transcend casual conversations.

From that point forward, our interactions grew more frequent and meaningful. We delved into a myriad of topics, immersing ourselves in the rich tapestry of shared interests, dreams, and aspirations. With each passing day, our connection deepened, guided by the genuine understanding and empathy that blossomed between us.

We soon found ourselves crossing paths in various settings, our encounters becoming a delightful tapestry of chance meetings and planned rendezvous. In these moments, we reveled in the joy of shared experiences, embracing the opportunity to create memories together. As we explored different places and engaged in heartfelt conversations, our bond strengthened, cementing the foundation of a friendship that seemed destined to endure.

Thus, through our initial encounter and the subsequent conversations that followed, we embarked on a journey of connection and companionship. It was a serendipitous meeting that defied the odds, leading us to discover kindred spirits in each other. From that moment forward, our lives became intertwined, as we continued to talk, share, and support one another, crafting a friendship that surpassed the boundaries of time and place.

An invisible force drew us closer together, diminishing the distance that once separated us. With every interaction and every shared moment, we delved deeper into each other's lives, unraveling the layers that concealed our true selves. Our connection transcended the realm of casual acquaintanceship, transforming into an integral and cherished bond that became an indispensable part of our existence.

In the tapestry of our growing friendship, trust blossomed like a delicate flower, its petals unfurling to reveal the depths of our shared experiences, hopes, and fears. We became confidants, offering solace and support in times of need, and celebrating the triumphs and joys that life bestowed upon us. Our conversations became a safe haven, a sanctuary where we could bare our souls without judgment or reservation.

Through laughter and tears, shared stories, and heartfelt conversations, we discovered the intricacies and nuances that made each of us unique. Our interests and passions intertwined, becoming a source of inspiration and encouragement for one another. We embarked on adventures together, exploring the world around us with newfound enthusiasm, knowing that our friendship was a steadfast anchor amidst the uncertainties of life.

Our connection became a lifeline, a source of strength and comfort during both the tranquil moments and the storms we encountered along our respective journeys. We leaned on each other, drawing courage from the unwavering support and understanding that flowed freely between us. Our friendship became a testament to the transformative power of human connection, reminding us of the beauty and resilience that lie within the bonds we forge.

As our souls intertwined, our friendship blossomed into something profound and enduring. It became a constant presence, a guiding light that illuminated our paths and enriched our lives. Our shared experiences and the countless memories we created together wove themselves into the fabric of our existence, leaving an indelible imprint on our hearts.

In this ever - evolving dance of friendship, we found solace, inspiration, and a sense of belonging. Our connection had become an intrinsic part of who we were, a pillar of support that stood firm amidst the trials and tribulations of life. Through the ebb and flow of time, our friendship had proven its resilience, reminding us that true companionship knows no bounds and can withstand the tests of distance and time.

In the tapestry of our lives, our friendship has become a vibrant thread, weaving its way through every moment and coloring our experiences with joy, love, and unwavering companionship.

As the impending first - semester exams loomed on the horizon, our focus shifted towards the realm of academia. With diligent determination, we immersed ourselves in our studies, preparing ourselves for the challenges that awaited us. Surprisingly, the journey of learning and academic growth proved to be more manageable than I had initially anticipated. The concepts began to align, and my understanding deepened, fostering a sense of confidence and calmness within me.

Amidst the flurry of textbooks, notes, and late-night study sessions, a reassuring tranquility enveloped me. The hard work and dedication we invested in our studies paid off, reflected in our preparation and performance. As the exams approached, a sense of assurance washed over me, replacing anxiety with a quiet optimism that whispered of impending success. It went well, and we had a gap of two weeks before next semester started.

Two weeks are too short to visit our home town, so we took a collective decision to organize a picnic that would bring together all of our batch mates. To my delight, Sonam's class also joined us, infusing the gathering with an extra spark of excitement. The anticipation of spending quality time with Sonam at the picnic sent a wave of exhilaration coursing through me.

Throughout the day, our paths intertwined, and serendipitous moments seemed to conspire to keep us in each other's company. The shared laughter, meaningful conversations, and shared experiences drew us closer, nurturing a sense of familiarity and connection that grew with each passing moment. I found myself irresistibly drawn to Sonam, her presence becoming a beacon that illuminated my heart.

As the day progressed, I became increasingly aware of deepening attraction I felt towards her. Every interaction, every shared smile, kindled a desire to spend more time in her presence and unravel the mysteries of our connection. The unspoken bond we shared, infused with moments of joy and shared experiences, kindled a flame within me, fanning the flames of affection and fondness.

For now, I nurtured these blossoming feelings, cherishing every stolen glance and cherished moment we shared. I held onto the hope that the stars would align, granting me the courage to express the depths of my affection when the time was right. The journey of love remained a clandestine one, hidden within the chambers of my heart, awaiting the perfect moment to unfurl its petals and bask in the light of truth.

In the meantime, I relished every opportunity to be near Sonam, cherishing the growing connection between us. I treasured the shared moments, committing them to memory as cherished tokens of our budding relationship. And as I carried the weight of my unspoken love, I remained hopeful that fate would guide us towards a future where our hearts could openly intertwine, and our love could bloom in full splendor.

Within the confines of a college nestled in a remote place, the passage of six months can feel like an eternity. In an environment where glimpses of a familiar and captivating face are a rarity, the longing for connection and companionship grows ever more intense. Unfortunately, the seclusion of our college did not shield us from the rampant whispers of gossip that permeated its halls.

Like the countless narratives that unfold within the walls of educational institutions, rumors began to take root and spread like wildfire. One of my batchmates, seemingly driven by envy and a desire to manipulate the situation to his advantage, initiated a campaign of misinformation. He aimed to cast shadows of doubt over the genuine connections that were blossoming between Sonam and me.

Driven by a deep-rooted longing for Sonam's affection, he sought to sow seeds of misunderstanding and mistrust. His actions were fueled by a sense of entitlement, as he harbored the hope that the fragile bonds we had formed would falter, creating an opportunity for him to step in and seize the affection he believed was rightfully his.

Amidst the chaos of these baseless rumors, the air became heavy with tension and uncertainty. It was disheartening to witness the impact of these malicious whispers on our fledgling relationship. The camaraderie and trust we had fostered faced an unexpected challenge, threatened by the poisonous tendrils of deceit and manipulation.

Yet, despite the turmoil, we remained steadfast in our connection, refusing to succumb to the falsehoods that swirled around us. Our bond, nurtured by genuine intentions and shared experiences, withstood the onslaught of rumors, emerging stronger in the face of adversity.

While the rumors brought moments of doubt and confusion, they also served as a stark reminder of the power of our connection. They revealed the lengths to which others were willing to go to disrupt our budding romance, affirming authenticity of the feelings we held for one another.

In the face of these challenges, we chose to rise above the fray, holding onto our trust in one another and the sincerity of our connection. We refused to let the actions of others define our relationship, knowing that our love and understanding would prevail over the whispers of deception.

Amidst the swirl of rumors, we remained resolute in our commitment to one another, determined to navigate the storms that threatened to engulf us. Together, we faced the waves of uncertainty, united in our resolve to protect the fragile flame of our love from the gusts of falsehood and manipulation.

These rumors started causing a rift between us, and it felt as though our friendship was slowly falling apart. I was left shattered to see how a small rumor could split our friendship. How these small things matter over the friendship and comfort I offered all this time. This was not easy for me, and I started being sad, and most of the time my tears flowed out without me being aware of them. The truth had been twisted, and my expectations had been shattered. We both stopped talking.

In the ceaseless flow of time, moments slipped through our fingers like grains of sand, each one carrying with it the weight of our shared journey. With unwavering determination, I sought to dismantle the web of deceit spun by Vineet, and assure Sonam that the rumors he had maliciously propagated held no truth.

I poured my heart into convincing her, offering reassurances that our connection was pure and untainted by the falsehoods that had tainted our reputation. I spoke from a place of sincerity, sharing my deepest emotions and baring my soul, hoping that my words would serve as a shield against the doubts and insecurities that threatened to erode our bond.

But despite my heartfelt efforts, the seeds of doubt had already been planted. The tendrils of suspicion had wrapped themselves around Sonam's thoughts, casting a shadow over the trust we had cultivated. The insidious impact of Vineet's deception had taken hold, and it proved challenging to dismantle the walls that had been erected within Sonam's heart.

The weight of my words seemed insufficient to counteract the lingering echoes of the rumors that had circulated. I watched with a heavy heart as Sonam wrestled with her emotions, torn between the whispers of deception and the connection we had nurtured.

In this struggle, I remained steadfast, refusing to let our love be defined by the fabrications of others. I persisted in my efforts to prove the authenticity of our relationship, providing unwavering support, understanding, and patience. I hoped that with time, Sonam would come to recognize the truth and find solace in the constancy of our love.

Yet, it was a challenging path to tread, as the wounds inflicted by rumors ran deep. It required immense strength and perseverance to dismantle the walls of doubt and rebuild the trust that had been shaken. I held onto the belief that love, when grounded in truth and nurtured by genuine intentions, has power to overcome even the most persistent doubts.

As the days melted into one another, the initial exhilaration and enthusiasm that had accompanied the start of the college journey began to wane. The spark that had once ignited my spirit and propelled me forward had flickered and dimmed. The second semester had arrived, but my once eager anticipation had been replaced by a pervasive sense of apathy and disillusionment.

Mornings became a struggle as I grappled with the desire to remain cocooned in the comfort of my bed, reluctant to face the challenges that awaited me beyond the confines of my room. My phone became a constant companion, its presence always within my line of sight, an ever - vigilant sentinel for any sign of connection or acknowledgement.

On the day of my birthday, my heart held a glimmer of hope, yearning for a call or a greeting from Sonam, a gesture that would reaffirm our bond amidst the growing darkness within me. However, disappointment washed over me as the day unfolded without the anticipated acknowledgement from her. The weight of sadness settled in, growing heavier with each passing moment.

In my search for solace, I turned to the allure of smoking, seeking temporary respite from the emotional turmoil that consumed me. It became a coping mechanism, a misguided attempt to numb the pain and find temporary reprieve from the depths of my sorrow. However, the relief was fleeting, and the emptiness remained.

As the months dragged on, the cloud of melancholy lingered, refusing to dissipate. The days blended together, with each passing moment echoing the monotony of my existence. The cycle seemed unbroken, and the landscape of my emotions remained unchanged.

The weight of desolation bore down upon me, obscuring the light of hope that had once burned within. The lack of connection and the absence of Sonam's presence in my life only deepened the sense of isolation, amplifying the despair that had taken root within me.

Four months slipped through my fingers, seemingly lost in the endless expanse of time, yet the situation remained stagnant. The yearning for change, for a flicker of joy to illuminate the shadows, grew stronger with each passing day. The once vibrant landscape of college life had faded, leaving behind a desolate emptiness that permeated my every thought.

In this abyss, I longed for a glimmer of light, a sign that would guide me out of the depths of my sorrow and towards a renewed sense of purpose. Hope whispered in the recesses of my heart, reminding me that even in the darkest times, there is the potential for transformation and healing.

I tried to get support from my friends, but nothing worked. I felt disturbed and unable to find peace anywhere. This is when I started drinking, too. I hardly get to see her. I started going to all those places we used to meet but have not seen her anymore.

All my attempts to talk to her were futile. I was lost in my thoughts, and the photos of her I had, were the only thing I would have my eyes stuck to.

Amidst the backdrop of my desolate emotional state, the practical realities of life beckoned. To sustain myself and fuel my newfound habits, I made the decision to seek employment and venture into the realm of part-time work. Embracing the role of a salesman in a shoe shop, I embarked on a journey of financial self-sufficiency.

The necessity of my circumstances compelled me to take charge of my own financial responsibilities. My parents, burdened with their own struggles, could no longer shoulder the weight of supporting me through this challenging phase. It was a bittersweet realization, but one that ignited a sense of determination within me to carve my own path.

Within the confines of the shoe shop, I found a refuge, a realm where I could temporarily escape the grip of my current situation. The interaction with customers, the meticulous arrangement of products, and the pursuit of sales became a welcomed distraction from the heaviness that weighed upon my soul.

Engaging in work offered a semblance of balance, providing structure and purpose to my days. The demands of the job allowed me to redirect my focus, at least momentarily, from the disheartening circumstances that had enveloped my college life. It was an opportunity to embrace a sense of productivity and independence as I sought to establish my own financial stability.

The demands of my part-time work served as a valuable distraction, redirecting my attention towards tangible goals and responsibilities. It became a balancing act where the pursuit of financial independence intertwined with the pursuit of personal growth and resilience.

In the midst of my daily interactions within the shoe shop, I found respite from the sadness that had enveloped me. The camaraderie with my colleagues and the satisfaction of contributing to my own well-being offered moments of reprieve, shielding me from the weight of my current situation.

"Breakups are not very easy, and that too this early in your relationship," said Ankit with a very deep voice. It looked like he was deep in the story. "Anyway, please continue, I am eager to know the rest," he said.

It was July 3rd, and it was Sonam's birthday. My heart wanted me to be with her, take her out, and make this day memorable for her. But I feared that she would not like it, and I stopped myself. I waited for seven days and finally mustered up the courage to call her. I wished her a happy birthday, but all Sonam said was, "Don't call me back, ever."

This response shattered me, and I realized that the friendship had come to an end. It was not easy for me to digest this, but I knew that I had to move on. I learned that sometimes friendships and relationships end, but memories remain forever, and living for these memories is worth more than living with the individual. At least you will have sweet memories of this.

As the hands of time continued their relentless march, four more months slipped away, their passing marked by a sense of repetitive monotony. The familiar faces, the mundane classes, the routine visits to the shoe shop, and the ever - present professors remained constants in the backdrop of college life. Yet, amidst this unchanging landscape, a palpable shift had taken place: Sonam had retreated into the realm of silence and inexpressiveness.

Over time, Sonam's frustration grew, fueled by the mentality of the people around her and the stifling atmosphere of the small town. The weight of these challenges became overwhelming, making it increasingly difficult for her to find solace and connection within the confines of our college. The incessant tug of homesickness, the struggle to adapt to a new environment, and the longing for a more supportive and nurturing community began to take their toll on her spirit.

Eventually, in a moment of clarity and determination, Sonam made the difficult decision to leave the college behind and return to her native place. Her parents supported this decision, and she embarked on the path of finding solace and peace away from the stifling confines of the small town that had failed to nurture her spirit.

The news of Sonam's departure, delivered by her roommate in the hostel, struck my heart with a sharp and piercing ache. The weight of sadness settled upon me, and I found myself unable to bear the pain of witnessing her go. In that moment, a surge of emotions consumed me, and a desperate longing took hold-to fly to her, to implore her to reconsider, to reverse the course of our journey.

The time we had lost, the moments of silence and distance, the hours she spent in the town alone, weighed heavily on my soul. I yearned for a chance to make amends, to bridge the chasm that had separated us, and to reclaim the precious moments we had allowed to slip away. Accepting this as the end was a bitter pill to swallow, and my heart rebelled against the notion, refusing to accept the finality of her departure.

I mustered the courage to call Sonam on the eve of her departure, clinging to the hope of a final conversation, a chance to express the depths of my feelings one last time. However, my attempts to connect were met with a resounding silence. Sonam deliberately disconnected each call, leaving my heart heavy with unspoken words and a longing that refused to be extinguished.

Undeterred by this setback, I refused to relinquish my pursuit of closure and understanding. Gathering my thoughts and summoning the strength within, I recorded a heartfelt voicemail, pouring my emotions into every word. I bared my soul, expressing all that had remained unspoken and assuring her that I would forever be a pillar of support, standing by her side whenever she needed.

As December 23, 2004, dawned, the day of her departure, a heavy cloud of melancholy hung in the air. Sonam left the college without uttering a goodbye, leaving me with a profound sense of loss and a lingering ache in my heart. It was a moment of finality, a painful realization that our paths had diverged, perhaps never to converge again.

In the wake of her absence, I grappled with a maelstrom of emotions - grief, regret, and a lingering hope that somehow, someday, our paths would cross once more. The void left by her departure echoed within me, a constant reminder of the depths of our connection and the weight of the unfinished chapters that lay between us.

As the college moved forward, the halls that once teemed with shared laughter and whispered promises felt emptier, haunted by memories of a love that had slipped through my fingers. Yet, in the depths of my being, a glimmer of resilience remained, whispering that love, in all its complexities and uncertainties, had the power to transform and reunite.

"This cannot end this soon, and I cannot believe this to be the end," interrupted Arjun. "Why have you let her go and not stopped her?" he added.

"Sometimes life has something else stored for us, and we need to be patient enough to reach there to enjoy what life is offering," added Rohan. "This is, for sure, not the end," he continued.

With Sonam's departure, a chapter of our lives came to an end, leaving behind a bittersweet residue of memories and experiences. The realization settled upon me that people, even those we hold dear, can drift apart as the currents of life carry us along separate paths. Goodbyes, it seemed, were an unavoidable part of our journey.

Yet, amidst the ache of parting, a flicker of hope ignited within me. I held onto the belief that true friendships, built on a foundation of genuine connection and shared experiences, possess an enduring spirit that transcends the bounds of time and distance. Though we were physically separated, I knew deep within my heart that the bond we shared with Sonam would never truly fade.

In the recesses of my soul, I nurtured the hope that one day our paths would converge once more, that destiny would weave its threads and grant us the opportunity to reconnect. Time, that gentle healer, had the power to mend wounds, bridge distances, and rekindle the flame of friendship that once burned bright.

I clung to the belief that the beautiful memories we had woven together would serve as a guiding light, leading us back to one another when the timing was right. Though the road ahead was uncertain, I nurtured the flame of anticipation, patiently awaiting the moment when our paths would intertwine again and we would have the chance to relive the treasured moments we had shared.

As the months drifted by, a new wave of technological advancement swept through India, bringing with it the rising popularity of the internet. Email and chatrooms emerged as conduits of connection, bridging the distances that separated us from our loved ones. Within the confines of our college, an internet lab came into existence, granting us the privilege of accessing this digital realm to communicate with our families and friends.

I managed to get Sonam's email address, and I found solace in this newfound avenue of expression. With every keystroke, I poured my heart out to her, sharing the depths of my emotions and offering sincere apologies for any past mistakes. Undeterred by the absence of a response, I persisted, sending her an email each day, meticulously chronicling the events and emotions that colored my existence.

Though aware that her reply might never arrive, I continued to bare my soul in each correspondence, finding solace in the writing. The words flowed from within, carrying with them the weight of my emotions - a cathartic release that eased the burden of guilt and longing. Through these heartfelt missives, I sought to bridge the divide and resurrect the connection that had once flourished between us.

Time passed by, but Sonam remained resolute in her stance, reaffirming her inability to see me as anything more than a friend. Her responses, or lack thereof, echoed the boundaries she had set, a gentle yet firm reminder that our paths had diverged and our feelings were not aligned.

Yet, despite the disheartening reality, I persevered in pouring my heart onto the digital canvas of each email. Each day, I shared the intricate tapestry of my life, entrusting Sonam with my hopes, dreams, and the minutiae of my daily experiences. In the act of writing, I found a sanctuary, a space where the weight of my unspoken emotions could be released, even if they remained suspended in the realm of one-sided communication.

Sonam's steadfastness served as a bittersweet reminder that sometimes, despite our deepest desires, the heart's journey takes unexpected turns. It was a lesson in acceptance - embracing the boundaries that had been set while still nurturing the flame of hope that friendship would endure.

And so, with unwavering determination, I continued to send those emails, each one a testament to the unyielding nature of my emotions and the enduring bond I held with Sonam. Though her responses may never come, my solace in the act of writing continued, knowing that each word sent out into the digital expanse carried a piece of my soul.

In the dance between hope and acceptance, I learned to navigate the intricate terrain of unrequited love. I held onto the beauty of our friendship, cherishing the memories we had shared while simultaneously embracing the reality of our divergent paths. And through it all, I started enjoying the power of expression, in the act of writing those daily emails, knowing that even in the absence of reciprocation, my words had the capacity to touch hearts and forge connections, no matter the distance that lay between us.

After patiently persevering with my heartfelt emails, a moment of triumph and joy graced my inbox as Sonam's response finally arrived. In her heartfelt message, she revealed the profound impact my emails had on her life. She confessed that she began each day by immersing herself in my email, finding relief and comfort in the connection we shared. The emails had become an indispensable part of her daily routine, a lifeline to our shared memories and emotions.

Sonam expressed her desire to respond, to reciprocate the emotions that had welled up within her, but found herself grappling with the words to begin. She acknowledged that her previous behavior had been misguided, and she offered a sincere apology for any pain it had caused. In a beautiful twist of fate, she revealed that she was returning to Rayagada for a brief visit, and she suggested that we meet once again.

A wave of elation washed over me as I read her words. The prospect of seeing her once more filled me with nervous excitement. Memories, both cherished and bittersweet, flooded my mind, painting a vivid tapestry of our shared journey. From the moment our eyes first met to the moments we spent together, and even the painful day of her departure, every precious memory danced before my eyes. The emotions overwhelmed me, causing tears of joy and nostalgia to well up within me.

And then, in a breathtaking moment, Sonam emerged from the train, stepping onto the platform with that same enchanting smile and magnetic allure in her eyes. Time seemed to halt, and the world around me faded into a blur. My focus narrowed, fixating solely on her radiant presence. In that moment, it felt as if the universe conspired to bring us together, and everything else dissolved into insignificance.

My heart surged with an overwhelming desire to run toward her, to embrace her in a tender hug, and to whisk her away from the rest of the world. I yearned to keep her by my side for eternity, to protect and cherish her. It felt as though my entire life had led up to this moment, as if I had been granted the privilege of living in this precious instant. If this were to be my last moment, I knew deep within that I wouldn't harbor any complaints.

In that captivating encounter, time regained its momentum, and the world resumed its bustling rhythm. But within my heart, an eternal flame had been ignited. The joy of reunion and the promise of rediscovering our connection infused every breath I took. The prospect of spending time with Sonam once again filled me with an indescribable sense of bliss as I eagerly awaited the adventures and conversations that awaited us.

With gratitude and an unwavering determination to savor each moment, I embarked on this chapter of our journey, knowing that life had granted us a precious second chance.

The day we had longed for finally arrived, and we spent it together, immersed in heartfelt conversations and joyful laughter that echoed the fondness of our past. Seizing the opportunity to share the depths of my emotions, I confessed to Sonam the profound impact she had on my life and the undeniable love that bloomed within my heart. With unabashed honesty, I recounted the moments that had unfolded since her departure, laying bare my experiences and the profound longing that had consumed me in her absence.

Moved by the sincerity of my words, Sonam reciprocated, revealing her own hidden feelings that had remained nestled within her heart. She confessed that her love for me had endured, even in the face of separation.

In that sacred moment, our connection deepened, and the seeds of a beautiful relationship were sown.

However, this was a short trip, and Sonam has to soon depart from Rayagada. This loomed on the horizon, an inevitable parting that would take her away once again. But this time, there was a newfound promise between us-a promise to remain in touch and nurture our connection through daily conversations and unwavering support.

As the days unfolded, our love continued to flourish, transcending the physical distance that separated us. Phone calls became the lifeline that sustained our relationship, bridging the gap between our hearts. However, with this newfound connection came the financial strains of increased phone bills and the added expense of maintaining our communication.

In an effort to accommodate these expenses, I made sacrifices, forgoing my own lunch to save money and diligently juggling the budget for both my conversations with Sonam and my personal indulgences. Balancing these financial demands alongside my part-time job became a delicate dance as I navigated the various facets of my life to ensure our love remained nurtured and cherished.

While it meant making certain adjustments and sacrifices, I embraced these challenges willingly, fueled by the knowledge that our connection was worth every penny. The joy of conversing with Sonam, of sharing our thoughts, dreams, and laughter, became a priceless treasure that transcended monetary concerns.

In the realm of love, I discovered a willingness to go the extra mile, to make sacrifices, and to reshape my priorities. And in return, I found fulfillment and happiness, knowing that our love was nurtured and nourished by our unwavering commitment to one another.

Together, we started the journey that spanned beyond the boundaries of distance and financial constraints, guided by the shared belief that our love was worth every ounce of effort and sacrifice. And in the tapestry of our relationship, we weaved a story of resilience, devotion, and the transformative power of love.

Sonam started her new course as a B-Pharma student in Delhi. She made a deliberate choice to embrace the independence that college life offered. Despite her parents residing in the same city, she opted to immerse herself in the hostel experience, savoring the taste of self-reliance and the exploration of life on her own terms. Though she visited her family periodically, she cherished the newfound freedom that independent living provided.

Amidst Sonam's pursuit of independence, our connection remained steadfast. We continued our regular communication, conversing over phone calls and exchanging messages that bridged the distance between us. While we had not yet formalized our commitments, my unwavering dedication was evident in the daily phone calls I made, eagerly awaiting the opportunity to hear her voice and engage in heartfelt conversations. Each day unfolded with the reassurance that our connection remained strong, and I nurtured the hope of a future where our love could bloom freely.

Time passed harmoniously as I juggled between my studies, my part-time job, and the precious moments spent conversing with Sonam. It felt as though I had stepped into a dreamlike paradise, where the rhythm of life flowed smoothly, guided by the currents of love and shared aspirations.

In another event, I received a call from Sonam. Her voice carried a sense of worry and turmoil as she confided in me, revealing that she had been unjustly accused of wrongdoing and was now facing legal charges. With a heavy heart, she admitted that she had no one else to turn to for help and implored me to come to her aid.

Concern coursed through my veins as I absorbed her plea. Though she had never asked for such assistance before, I knew that this was a moment of dire need, and I couldn't bear to see her suffer alone. Sonam shared her apprehension about involving her parents in the situation, fearing the repercussions it would bring. Without a second thought, I assured her of my unwavering support, vowing to be by her side through the ordeal.

In order to reach her side swiftly, I had to make the arduous journey from Rayagada to Bhubaneswar, where I would board a flight to Delhi. However, the financial aspect of this endeavor weighed heavily on my mind. Despite reaching out to friends, I found that the sum of money I required eluded me. Faced with limited options,

I made the difficult decision to part with the sentimental gold chain my mother had gifted me before I began college. Selling it provided the means to proceed with my mission to aid Sonam.

With determination coursing through my veins, I boarded the next train and embarked on a journey that would bring me to Delhi. During my stay, I sought refuge with a friend and dedicated myself to assisting Sonam, both emotionally and in her legal battle. Each passing day was marked by unwavering commitment as I marshaled every resource at my disposal to prove her innocence, provide the support she needed, and stand as her unwavering pillar of strength.

As the clock ticked, I remained steadfast in my pursuit to alleviate her distress, knowing that my presence and dedication were indispensable in her fight for justice. Lucky for me, I knew someone in Delhi who was also practicing as a lawyer in the Delhi court. After persistent efforts and with the assistance of my friends, we managed to clear Sonam's name from the case that had unjustly plagued her. The weight of the false accusations dissipated with the assurance that no trace of her involvement would remain in any records.

Sonam's heart overflowed with joy and gratitude for my unwavering support throughout the ordeal. She began to truly comprehend the depth of my care and devotion, and a newfound appreciation bloomed within her.

In the wake of this triumph, a bittersweet mix of emotions enveloped me. I reveled in the satisfaction of knowing that I had done everything in my power to aid Sonam and guide her toward freedom from the fabricated entanglement. Yet, the loss of the cherished gift my mother had bestowed upon me served as a poignant reminder of the sacrifices made along the way.

Curiosity tugged at my heart, compelling me to inquire about the circumstances that had led to this turbulent situation. Sonam revealed the unfolding of events during her time in Delhi, where she crossed paths with a man named Naveen. Their initial encounters had sparked a relationship characterized by late-night revelry, clubbing, and pub hopping, fueling a sense of excitement and adventure. However, as time progressed, Sonam stumbled upon Naveen's involvement in illicit activities, specifically his connections with local drug dealers and his reliance on unlawful sources of income.

When Sonam confronted Naveen about these troubling revelations, he initially evaded her inquiries, desperate to maintain the facade he had constructed. Eventually, under persistent questioning, he reluctantly admitted the truth, but his response was accompanied by threats and coercion, warning Sonam against exposing his shady dealings. Frightened and eager to sever ties with Naveen, Sonam found herself trapped in a web of forged accusations, a cruel ploy devised by Naveen to keep her ensnared.

At this tumultuous juncture, Sonam faced the daunting task of extricating herself from both the toxic relationship that still held lingering feelings and memories and the legal quagmire that had engulfed her. Left without support or guidance, she found strength in our growing bond, recognizing the unwavering dedication I had shown and the resilience we had cultivated together.

Through her unwavering trust and collaboration, we embarked on a joint journey to overcome the entanglement that threatened to shatter Sonam's life. It was a testament to the growing strength of our bond, solidified by our shared determination to emerge from the darkness hand in hand.

Following our victorious triumph, I returned to Rayagada, where our relationship blossomed with new found depth and meaning. Our connection transcended physical distance as we continued to spend cherished moments together, sharing our lives over the phone, embarking on memorable trips, and divulging our dreams and aspirations. Despite the mounting debts that burdened me, I kept my financial struggles concealed, determined to keep the flame of our love burning bright.

As my second year of college drew to a close, I eagerly anticipated the next chapter of our journey. Over a period of time, I marveled at the remarkable alignment of fate that repeatedly brought us together, even in moments of separation. Through the trials and tribulations that beset our relationship, the love we held for one another remained steadfast, a beacon of hope that illuminated our path.

Motivated by a deep longing to strengthen our connection, I made a decision that would change everything. I would propose to Sonam. I thought it would be better to go to Delhi and propose to her. I took the train and reached Delhi. I just had a day to spend in Delhi, and I had my return ticket for the same day. It was raining the day when I reached.

In the morning, I met Sonam, and together we indulged in the magic of a romantic movie. The enchantment lingered as we ventured to Delhi Haat, seeking solace in each other's company. Seated at a quiet table, savoring cups of coffee, we immersed ourselves in conversations about our future. Overwhelmed by an outpouring of emotions, I knew the time had come to profess my love to Sonam.

In an instant, I descended to one knee, extracting a small ring from the depths of my pocket. Sonam's surprise was evident, yet she sensed the gravity of the moment. Gazing deeply into her eyes, I whispered, "Sonam, you are the most extraordinary person in my life. I yearn to spend every moment by your side. Will you do me the honor of marrying me?"

The world seemed to hold its breath, suspending time as we awaited Sonam's response. In that fleeting moment, all the hopes, dreams, and cherished memories we had shared converged into a single question, seeking affirmation of a future bound by love.

As Sonam and I bid farewell to that rainy evening, our hearts intertwined with the knowledge that our lives were forever changed. With every step toward the train station, a bittersweet blend of happiness, love, and sadness accompanied us. We held each other's hands tightly, drawing strength from the connection we shared, cherishing the moments we had spent together.

A sense of contentment enveloped me, knowing that I had discovered my soulmate, someone I would go to great lengths to keep happy. The memory of that rainy afternoon in Delhi Haat etched itself into the depths of my heart, serving as a constant reminder of the profound love we had found.

Sonam became the beacon of light that illuminated my life, infusing it with happiness and positivity. The weight of the loans I had accrued weighed heavily on my shoulders, a constant reminder of the sacrifices I had made to keep our connection alive. Skipping meals, selling personal belongings, and relying on the generosity of friends were all part of the journey, ensuring that our love endured despite financial hardships.

College is over now, and I managed to get a job in sales, and I was happy as this is what I always wanted to do. Although the salary was not very great, I still started to collect experience. I moved to Pune for this job, and I was excited. I started earning and also used the money to repay some of the loans I took during college. I started working hard to ensure that I reached a salary level that could provide me with enough comfort in my life.

In December 2009, as Sonam approached the final year of her college studies, with a postponed exam providing a window of time, she decided to visit me in Pune. Eager to make every moment count, I devoted myself to working tirelessly, determined to settle my debts, cover the mounting phone bills, and make all the necessary arrangements for her arrival.

Our time together in Pune was nothing short of magical. We explored the vibrant city hand in hand, reveling in the joy of discovering new places together. From visiting temples and parks to indulging in movies and dining at restaurants, every experience felt heightened by the presence of our love. It was during our visit to Dagdu Seeth's temple that I marked a special moment of commitment, gently adorning her forehead with a red tikka-a gesture often reserved for married individuals in India. It symbolized the depth of our connection and the promise of a shared future.

Each moment became a treasure, and we embraced every opportunity to create lasting memories. However, as the end of our time together loomed, the ache of separation began to cast its shadow upon us. Yet, our love for one another served as an anchor, providing the strength needed to endure the pain. With hearts heavy, we embraced each other tightly at the railway station, the weight of emotion almost too much to bear. Tears streamed down my face as the train departed, carrying her away from me. In the midst of my sorrow, Sonam's text message reached me, offering solace and reassurance that our love would empower me to carry on.

I was sad after dropping her off at the railway station. I went to the office just after dropping her off. My boss, attuned to my emotional state, sensed my distress. With genuine concern, he urged me to take a break for the day, assuring me that everything would be alright. His kindness and understanding provided a glimmer of comfort during that challenging time.

That day served as a poignant reminder of the profound impact that love and separation can have on the human heart. The depth of our connection left an indelible mark on my soul, compelling me to persevere, fueled by the enduring power of our love.

As Sonam arrived in Delhi, our communication primarily relied on phone calls. Concerned about the rising telephone bills, we made the decision to acquire a Reliance SIM card, which offered more affordable rates during nighttime calls. With the new SIM card in hand, our conversations expanded from mere minutes to lengthy conversations lasting an hour. The deepening connection between us only grew stronger with each passing conversation.

Due to another postponement of her exam, Sonam saw an opportunity to celebrate the upcoming New Year together. Excitement filled the air as we eagerly planned to meet at the picturesque destination of Coorg. However, despite my overwhelming eagerness to see her once again, the financial constraints I faced hindered my ability to fully engage in the planning process. Aware of my predicament, Sonam astutely calculated that the tour expenses would not exceed Rs. 7000, while I estimated they would likely surpass Rs. 11,000. Through a night of extensive discussion, we meticulously ironed out all the details, deliberating until the early morning hours.

With the sun beginning to rise at 7:00 a.m., we finally arrived at a mutual decision. The desire to embark on this journey together outweighed the financial challenges, and we committed to seizing the opportunity that lay before us. As Sonam proceeded to book her ticket, exhaustion from our lengthy planning call consumed me, leaving me desperately in need of rest.

However, my slumber was abruptly interrupted by the persistent vibrations of my phone. A surge of panic coursed through me as I observed a staggering 32 missed calls from Sonam.

Hastily, I sprang out of bed and dialed her number, my mind racing with a multitude of worrisome thoughts. I anxiously inquired about her well-being, relief washing over me as I heard the calmness in her voice. Sonam joyfully shared the news that she had successfully secured a ticket, albeit for a bus journey. She went on to explain that the bus route was not direct and would pass through Bangalore, adding an additional 10 hours of travel time. Despite the extended journey, she expressed her excitement and willingness to endure the discomfort in order to be together. It was the best option available within our limited budget. With the necessary funds gathered and her bags packed, she embarked on her voyage.

Returning to bed, I sought solace in a rejuvenating sleep, eager to be well-rested upon her arrival. Throughout her journey, we maintained a continuous stream of communication whenever network connectivity permitted, cherishing each opportunity to connect and share our experiences.

After a brief nap to replenish her energy, Sonam braced herself for the forthcoming 15 hour journey. Our desire to spend time together amidst the enchanting mountains of Coorg guided our choice of destination. The budgetary constraints we faced were alleviated by the presence of friends who graciously offered us accommodations. Boarding the bus around 10:00 p.m., our journey commenced. It was a Tuesday night, and we had packed a meal consisting of chicken and other treats.

At the stroke of midnight, we found ourselves enjoying dinner under the soft glow of the bus's dim lights, reminiscent of a romantic candlelit ambiance. Fatigue weighed heavily on Sonam, prompting me to encourage her to rest. Before surrendering to sleep, we exchanged a tender kiss, a momentary expression of our love, within the confines of the moving bus. As Sonam drifted off, nestled comfortably in my lap, I cradled her delicate form, overwhelmed with a sense of protective tenderness. Gazing at her serene countenance, tears welled in my eyes, and for the next two hours, I remained captivated by her presence before eventually succumbing to slumber. The journey went well, and we had a nice time together.

Sonam went back to Delhi and waited to finish the exam so that she could move to Pune for her internship. Luckily, she got a place in Pune, and she called me to inform me of this. I was excited that we could live together in Pune. I was excited that her presence in my town would give us enough opportunity to be together, strengthening the bond we shared. We eagerly anticipated the completion of her exams, as it would mark the beginning of her stay with me. We engaged in detailed discussions about her accommodation arrangements, and she too expressed her desire to reside with me. Initially, I was thrilled by her decision, but as reality set in, I grew concerned about the financial implications.

Transitioning from a shared room to a rented flat solely on my salary would be a significant adjustment. Sonam's internship would not provide a high income, further adding to my worries. Despite the practical considerations, I found it impossible to say no. Her radiant smile held me captive, compelling me to take on the responsibility of ensuring her well-being.

I dedicated myself to securing a suitable apartment within my limited budget for us to stay together. Although it may not have been the most luxurious option available, I strived to transform it into a welcoming home for Sonam. When the day arrived, I eagerly picked her up from the airport, both excited to step into our small apartment that we could decorate and personalize according to our tastes. We designated our respective corners, carefully selecting colors for the curtains and walls to create a space that truly felt like our own. Discussions on kitchenware and the division of household responsibilities ensued, and I willingly embraced each decision.

Despite the knowledge that these additional expenses would strain my already meager budget, I couldn't resist her infectious smile. It captivated me, rendering me unable to utter the word "no." I understood that sacrifices would be necessary, and I prepared myself to forgo meals and rely on public transportation, opting for the bus instead of my bike. Every penny saved would be significant, as I recognized that this was just the beginning of our journey together.

Despite the initial excitement of living together after years of long-distance dating, the reality of our differences began to surface, putting our relationship to the test. Sonam had always had a taste for the finer things in life, while I had financial constraints that limited my ability to indulge in such luxuries. Although I had a decent job in sales, the burden of loans and financial obligations made it difficult for me to meet Sonam's extravagant expectations.

In the beginning, Sonam didn't seem bothered by our financial disparities. We were content simply being together and exploring our new surroundings. However, over time, she started dropping hints about wanting more expensive gifts and outings, which I couldn't afford. Initially, I tried to brush off these hints, hoping they were just passing remarks. However, they persisted, and it became clear that this was becoming a significant issue in our relationship.

One day, while strolling through a mall, Sonam's eyes fell upon a designer perfume that caught her attention. It came with a hefty price tag that exceeded my monthly budget. I mustered up the courage to explain that it was beyond our means, but Sonam refused to accept my explanation. She became upset, accusing me of not caring about her happiness. Our disagreement quickly escalated into a heated argument, and I found myself taken aback by the sudden turn of events. It was disheartening to witness the strain that financial disparities were placing on our relationship.

As the strain in our relationship grew, I came to a difficult realization. It became clear that our visions of life and our priorities were misaligned. While I believed in financial responsibility and living within our means, Sonam desired a more extravagant and lavish lifestyle that I simply couldn't provide.

Despite my efforts to explain our financial limitations, Sonam seemed unwilling or unable to comprehend the situation. She continued to express her dissatisfaction and disappointment, making me feel inadequate and guilty for not meeting her expectations. The accusations of being spineless and incapable of taking care of her wishes only added to the emotional turmoil.

In the midst of this ongoing conflict, I began to understand that our relationship had become toxic. The constant focus on money and materialistic desires had overshadowed the love and happiness we once shared. It was a painful realization, but I knew that for the sake of my own well-being and emotional health, something had to change.

One day, Sonam had an accident and broke her leg. I took care of her, paid for all the medical expenses, and even took a break from my job to be with her. But things started to take a different turn. Sonam began treating me as an unknown person, and I felt like a stranger in my own home. She started talking to someone on the phone constantly, and I couldn't help but cry in the bathroom while listening to their conversations.

I tried to talk to Sonam and sort things out, but she wasn't interested. She had found herself a new friend - someone who would listen to her and cater to her every whim. I felt helpless and alone. However, I couldn't abandon her in her time of need, so I continued to take care of her until she recovered.

Once Sonam was back on her feet, I knew it was time to end things between us. I couldn't continue living in a loveless relationship, and I couldn't take the emotional pain anymore. I asked her to move out, and I also moved out of the apartment to start a new life.

I learned an important lesson from this experience. Never to be without money in my life. I realized that money is important for survival, and without it, life can become very challenging. I started to work harder, save money, and invest it wisely. It has been years since that incident, but I still remember it like it happened yesterday. It taught me to be strong, independent, and financially stable.

I changed jobs after this and dedicated myself to earning a good living. Good enough to not get into the situation I was in so far. Day in and day out, from one opportunity to another, I started climbing the ladder in corporate and eventually became the youngest sales director in the company. I also closed a few impossible deals for the company and have received heavy incentives in return. I invested all my money in the market and got good returns. Luck was with me. Soon, I became an angel investor and invested in some of the most successful startups in India, and the money I invested grew many folds.

I also took up the hobby of trekking and mountaineering as an escape from my hard - working life. This was my escape from life, and I used to take at least 2-3 breaks a year. On one such trip, I met Radhika, and we gelled well. She was also a yoga instructor and helped me find mental stability within myself. We dated for a few years before I proposed to her for marriage, and she agreed. The rest is all history.

Chapter 4
Love In A Small Town

"So a happy life at the end," said Nikhil to Rohan.

"Yes, it's all happy in the end," responded Rohan.

"Are you still in touch with her?" Do you talk to her often? Do you stalk her on social media yet? Asked Arjun, jokingly.

"Yes, we are in touch, and we often talk too. It feels good."

"You are lucky, Rohan," said Nikhil. "Not everyone is as lucky as you are."

"Why?" "Who is stopping you from following up?" said Rohan in a funny voice.

"I can't, even if I wish to do so," said Nikhil. "She is no more in this world," he added.

Everyone went silent all of a sudden. "We are sorry." We didn't mean to hurt you, said Rishi and everyone echoed him.

"There's nothing to be sorry for," Nikhil said, recounting his love story, which has forever changed him and his life. He began to describe the small town where he was raised.

Dantewada is where it all started. It's a district located in the state of Chhattisgarh in central India, known for its natural beauty and rich cultural heritage. The district is home to dense forests, hills, rivers, and waterfalls, making it an ideal destination for nature lovers and adventure seekers. Indravati National Park and Kanker Valley National Park are two prominent natural attractions in the district, where visitors can witness a variety of wildlife, including tigers, leopards, elephants, and rare species of birds and reptiles.

Because there are few central government iron ore mines in the district, it is fairly cosmopolitan. This is where my father has his job and was posted. People from almost all the states of India live there. For the very same reason, it has also been grappling with the issue of naxalism for several years. The Naxalite movement is a left-wing extremist movement that seeks to overthrow the Indian government and establish a socialist state.

The Naxals have also been accused of extorting money from local businesses and disrupting development projects in the region. These insurgencies in Dantewada have resulted in significant violence, including attacks on government officials, security forces, and civilians. I am also a victim of this movement. I am not sure whether this is for good or bad, but all I know is that this has changed my world forever.

We had various types of residences in the project area. Type 1 is the lowest grade for low-level workers, and Type 5 is the highest office bearer in the project, with clubbing exclusively for them and their children. We were in a modest type 3 colony with all the basic amenities and a modest way of life.

I was almost 14 years old and about to enter adolescence. This is when many changes in the body started. All of a sudden, every girl in school and the colony started looking attractive. I'd like to be in places where I can see a lot of girls, which used to give me pleasure. A guilty pleasure, I assume.

Everyone in the town knew each other, and people were happy to meet each other. We used to go to anyone's house and ask for whatever we could eat. We used to celebrate the festivals together. There is no division of caste and religion. We used to live more like a family and attend each other's gatherings. In one such gathering, I saw a beautiful 12-to 13-year-old girl with her head covered, wearing a decent salwar kameez, with her parents. I learned that her father is a local leader for some political party with a high level of influence in the community. People described him as a good man, and he also looked the same. He was also naturally helpful.

I was only looking at the girl. From a safe distance where no one could see me, I was observing everything about her. I found that she has a very strong sense of faith and values, which are reflected in her behavior and interactions with others. She had a kind heart, a warm smile, and radiated positive energy. She is very confident and poised, yet humble and respectful. Her inner beauty shines through in her actions and words, and she was inspiring others with her compassion, generosity, and grace. Her face was glowing like the light of the moon, and she was giving me the coolness that the moon gives to the earth. I just wanted to keep looking at her and nothing else. I wanted the time to stop at that moment so that I could see her to my satisfaction.

When someone falls in love for the first time, it can be an intense and overwhelming experience, and they may find themselves thinking about their girlfriend frequently. I, too, have found something very similar. I wasn't sure if it was because of love or because of my age. Whatever it was, at least I was enjoying the moment. I was in a constant state of daydreaming, where I only used to think about her everywhere: in my class, on my school bus, in the playground, and even in my house sometimes.

I recently discovered that my appreciation for English songs has grown. I started hearing 'Hello' by Lionel Richie multiple times, especially the line where he sings the below line.

'I've been alone with you inside my mind.
And in my dreams, I've kissed your lips a thousand times.
I sometimes see you pass outside my door.
Hello, is it me you're looking for?
I started finding ways to be near her. I started finding all the details around her. Her school, her home, her friends, the places she goes to play, and the people she plays

with, have become places for me to be and people to be with. I just wanted to be near her and get noticed. I also found out about the tuition she used to go to, and I too started going to the same tuition. This is also where I learned her name. She went by the name Noor, and she was Muslim. Her name means "Divine Light," and she lived up to it. She was the divine light for me, at least. I also discovered that she is quite good at studying, which inspired me to study as well. I wanted to do everything I could to impress her.

This continued for months, and I started getting serious about my studies and many other things in life. I found her well - mannered and cultured. In her opinion, I must be well - mannered and cultured. She was also very courteous to others, and all of a sudden I am as well. My friends and family have noticed my transformation over the last few days. When you live in a small town, I'm sure you notice a lot of things. People watch everything, and they for sure need more and more topics for their gossip. This is the beauty of living in a small town, and I didn't want my episodes to be too obvious to everyone. It will not take much time for our parents to know about this, and soon this will turn into a communal war.

Board exams were near, so we all became serious about our studies. Life consisted of only school, tuition, and books, with occasional trips to places where I could see Noor. This has become my routine while preparing for the exam and also during exams. Post - examination, the same routine continued.

I never dared to talk to her. I knew that Muslim families are a little conservative when it comes to talking to boys and making friendships with them. I wanted to be respectful of this and didn't want to invite much trouble for myself or for her. After a few days, we passed our board exam with flying colors and decided to major in science. I wanted to be a software engineer and wanted to move to the USA to pursue my career and eventually settle there. This is the small life plan I have made for myself.

School started, and I was surprised to see Noor in my class in 11th grade. I was really happy to see this. Noor was also happy to see me. She was happy that she at least had some familiar faces at the school. We were in the same class. And I was happy that I would get to know Noor more now and that people would have no stories to tell. They will accept us as classmates, and we will have opportunities to spend time together.

All of a sudden, our eyes stopped at each other. "Hey, Nikhil," she said with a smile on her face.

"Hey, Noor, what a surprise!" I said to her. "what are you doing here?" I asked.

"I changed my school," she said. "This is near my home, and this school has a better reputation than my previous school," she further added.

"Well, that is great." Feel free to let me know if you need anything here. I added, with a confident voice, and we moved towards our respective places to sit in class. We were sitting in different rows in the class. I was excited from inside but hadn't revealed this to her. I just kept this to myself. I didn't want to demonstrate how desperate I was to be with her. I wanted this relationship to develop gradually so that it grew tastier and tastier than I had anticipated.

That was the day I discovered that Noor and I would be in the same class for the next two years. I was not only excited but also overly enthusiastic to attend this school. I never missed lessons after that. I was always the first one to arrive at school and probably the last one to leave.

Have I become studious all of a sudden? I bet not. I was just looking for more and more opportunities to be around Noor. I wanted to observe her. I wanted to understand her. I wanted to impress her, and in short, I wanted my life to revolve around them. Everything I was doing, I was doing to achieve this.

Was it helpful in the end? I can see that Noor has also started looking for me. At every break, she would come to me and start the discussion. We would go to the lunchroom together, we would go to the library together, and we would also participate in the cultural society of the school together. It looks like even more have started to like spending time with me.

I started feeling like I was in love. The love that is pure it's not a compulsion but a push from within to be with her. A push coming from within to see her happy. I wanted to make every effort to make her smile. This was not the kind of love that required a physical relationship; it was more of a mental one. It was more of a hard relationship where our eyes sometimes spoke more than we did.

Sometimes I felt that whenever I saw her, my heart started beating very fast, and there were butterflies in my stomach. It's an amazing feeling that comes with her, and you always wish that it continues. You start looking for options and opportunities, and you again go back to the same zone where your heart beats as fast as Shatabdi, and your body goes numb. The only thing that you remember is you and her in the beautiful world. Everything else around you becomes meaningless, and to some extent, it also goes out of your focus.

The days moved by, and our friendship started deepening. Deeper than before. We started spending a lot of time together. We started doing a lot of activities in school together, and we started finding each other whenever we had free time. We both wanted to spend more and more time together. It was not there; she was the only girl in the school or the only girl in the class, but there was something special in her that was attracting me every time. She was very pure, and as she talked, her innocence and purity were really felt.

I became so desperate and restless that I wanted to propose to her. I wanted to try my luck. I wanted to see the reaction from her side. I also wanted to understand if this was just a friendship or if there was some-thing more. I also wanted to understand whether I could continue living my dream life after school or if this would be the end of our lovely relationship.

One day, when we were at our cultural music festival and preparing the stage for the musical show, I found her alone in a corner and went to her. I started talking to her, and all of a sudden there was complete silence. I said nothing, and she also chose not to talk. There was silence for a while. This seems to be the biggest silence I have ever felt. I felt as if the moment had stopped, and there was nothing I wanted from this moment. We chose to leave this moment for a while before I broke my silence and told Noor I wanted to be with him forever and that I wanted this moment to never end. Can you decide to spend the rest of your life with me? I'm in love with you, and here I am on my knees asking for your love.

Noor was surprised and shocked by this reaction. It looks like she was not prepared for this. All of a sudden, her face turned red, and I could see that she was uncomfortable facing me. She said nothing. She stood there for a while, then left the place. The very next moment, I saw her taking her back and leaving for the day. I felt guilty, and this feeling of guilt stayed with me for the rest of the day. I was thinking, why have I done this? Is this move a relationship spoiler? Is this the end of our friendship? What will happen if she tells this to her parents or somebody else? You can see there were a lot of questions to be answered, and I was standing there surprised, shocked, and confused. I didn't sleep that night and was eagerly waiting for the day.

My eyes were swollen because I hadn't slept the whole night. As soon as I reached school, I started looking for Noor. I was relieved to see that she is in school today, and she's in a happy mood too. I gathered my courage and went to her to wish her well. I wished her a good morning and inquired as to why she had only left yesterday. She chose not to answer but just to smile. I insisted, and she told you to know the answer. This smile on her face was a very big relief for me. I understood that the situation was not as bad as I thought it would be. I also understood that she might not have told anybody about this and that I was safe. The class started, and the day started normally.

When we met during the lunch break, I asked her why she hadn't responded to my question. She told me, "You are a good boy, and I like spending time with you." "Given another opportunity, I would never like these days to be finished. I would also love to spend my life with you. I would also like to be with you forever. But this is a small place. Ours is a very small society, and moreover, you are a Hindu boy. I'm not allowed to look at something beyond my religion. We generally get married to our relatives, and you and I too will have to follow suit. I don't want to go against my parents, and I also don't want to bring a bad name to my parents and family. So it would be nice if we remained friends forever and shared the memories with each other like this."

Although I liked the response from Noor, I was not satisfied, and I was not convinced that someone would not be with someone just for religion. I asked her to think beyond religion for a while. Think that there's no barrier; it's just you and me without any labels on us. Will her response be the same?

She smiled and said no. If there is no barrier, my answer will not be the same. You are a good boy, Nikhil, and I would also love to spend the rest of my life with you. But I also want to be practical, and I also want my family to be with me in my decision. It's not that I have any problem with you or your religion; it's just that we're not compatible.

She was making complete sense to me, but I was not ready to accept that I would not be able to be with her for the rest of my life. I told her, "Let's be friends," or even better, "Let's be boyfriend and girlfriend." Let's leave our next one and a half years of life as if we had lived our entire lives. Let's not spoil our present thinking by thinking about the future. Who knows, someday we both may fly to a whole new world where no one cares what religion you come from and we will have the opportunity to be together as husband and wife. Who knows, things may change tomorrow, and people from our place may also become more open-minded. Who knows, this taboo will now become a socially acceptable act someday. Let's not waste time thinking about the future; let's be in the present. For today, all I know is that I am in love with you, as I told her, and I don't want this moment to end anytime soon.

She smiled and nodded her head, yes. She liked my idea and my proposal. She, too, agreed that it was a better way to spend our time. We chose to be in a relationship. We chose to at least believe that, but we are a couple, and we will live together forever. I was happy, and so was Noor, with this arrangement.

We, in our hearts, are couples now, but for the rest of the world, we still have to act as if nothing has changed. The world outside is still the same. The world inside us has changed, though. We started treating each other as though we were boyfriend and girlfriend. We also sometimes hold each other's hands when no one is around and leave them as soon as we sense someone.

We started respecting each other and also started telling each other our choices for clothes for the next day. We also started to meet in public parks and other public restaurants. We started spending as much time as we could, keeping in mind that we didn't have to be caught.

We also started spending more time together in chemistry and physics labs, which has helped me be more focused on my studies too. We used to exchange notes with each other and also clear each other's doubts in studies. This was another great feeling, as being with her is also helping me with my studies and making my grades better.

I invited Noor to my home once during Diwali. She was dressed in a traditional maroon salwar kurta. She was looking amazing and very traditional, too. Her brother too came with her because, in a small town, girls are not allowed to go to a boy's house all by themselves. Younger brothers are their guards, and wherever sisters go, they will have to follow them.

My mom initially did not know that her name is Noor and that she is a Muslim girl. She continued to look at her, as moms always do. I am sure she might also have dreamed of having a daughter-in-law. She smiled and asked if she was my girlfriend. I said a big no, and she asked then why only her and not other girls and boys from your class. I introduced Noor as my classmate and a good friend. I also told them that we study together, and that's why only she and not others. She believed my version of the story, but the spark in her eyes was telling me everything.

That was the first time Noor came to my house. She was a bit shy and touched the feet of my parents as soon as she entered. My dad wanted to know whose daughter she was, and I told him that she was the daughter of the local MLA. My dad also felt happy, as we have the MLA's daughter in our home as our guest.

We did puja that day and had dinner together. After dinner, my dad asked me to drop her at her place. I took the car out and drove her and her brother to their home. That was the first time she was in my car, and we drove together. I felt as if this was the new normal and she would always be with me. We will always drive together like this and go places like this. Well, I was in my dreams, and her home came. I dropped them and went back to my home with a smile glued to my face. I hardly slept that night. I was thinking of all the places Noor went and touched. I still feel her presence in the air and in my house. My parents also liked her for her being so simple and of course for her dad.

She also invited me to her home once for a local celebration at her place. Politicians keep throwing parts without any occasion too. I went to her home, and she introduced me to her parents. Her parents smiled and then excused themselves, as they had a house full of guests that they wanted to attend. We were left alone with her younger brother of course to keep an eye on us. She tricked him and sent him to go play with his friends. He ran away, and here we go-it's just the two of us in the lovely corner of her house, where everyone is busy attending to guests for the party.

I started talking, and all of a sudden she put her fingers in my lips as a symbol to keep quiet and not talk at all. She was silent, and I too went silent for some time. We were staring at each other for some time without uttering any words at all. Soon, we realized that we had started breathing heavily. We still stared at each other for some time. All of a sudden, we hugged each other, and there was our first kiss. We kissed for a very brief period, and then we realized that we were not in a great setting, so we parted. Noor ran away and to another corner, and I kept standing there. I was like lost, standing there, thinking about what had just happened a moment before. It took me a while to come back to my senses.

I can still feel her hugging and kissing me. I am not able to come out of it. The same scene stayed in my head, and the same scene kept repeating itself again and again in my head. While I was eating at the party, I still had the same scene running through my head. I was driving back to my home and still had the same scene in my head.

I reached home and went straight to bed without even talking to anyone. I was lying on my bed and trying to sleep, but with the scene playing over and over in my head, it was not easy. I didn't sleep the whole night and just kept thinking about the scene again and again. The night just went by, and I didn't sleep at all. It was already morning by now, and I didn't have any sleep in my eyes.

As the days progressed, I knew that this was not going to work this way. I need someone to discuss this and let this go out of my head. If this continues for some time, I feel as if I'll go mad. I was desperate to find someone to tell this to. I rushed to school, as I was sure I could not tell this to my parents. As soon as I got someone else to tell me this, I wanted this to go away from my mind. I reached the class and saw Noor in it. She was very normal, and she looked well rested. I can't see the same level of eagerness in her as I had. I was surprised and confused. Why is she looking so normal? Why is she not as restless as I am?

In order to kill my doubts, I thought to go to her directly and ask her directly. I asked her to come out and ask about what had happened last night. She acted so normally and said nothing. It's all normal, and she asked me to chill. I was confused further, but the naughty smile on her face gave me the answer. I knew that she was not going to tell me anything and that she would love to keep it a mystery. I too decided to keep this a secret and to keep it with me forever.

"What happened yesterday was divine and has united us from two to one." This is what she said, and she ran away from there. I was excited, and now I knew her feelings as well. I also know that I am not the only one who has this feeling. The comment about this being divine itself shows how holy she thinks this is. I chose the right girl for me, and we are truly made for each other.

While all this was happening between Noor and me, the Naxal movement began in Dantewada and started to become more vigorous. The long - standing grievances among the tribal communities in the region and their governments started becoming more and more difficult. These grievances were rooted in issues of land ownership, resource exploitation, and the marginalization of their traditional way of life. The Maoist insurgents, also known as Naxalites, took advantage of these grievances and began to mobilize the tribal communities in the area.

With the formation of the People's Liberation Guerrilla Army, the military wing of the Communist Party of India (Maoist), this movement started growing more and more. The PLGA began to carry out a series of attacks on government installations, police outposts, and security forces in the region. The attacks were aimed at destabilizing the government and establishing a Maoist regime in the region.

The Naxalites soon gained control of large parts of Dantewada, including several villages, and began to establish their own parallel government. They set up their own judicial system, imposed taxes on the local population, and used force to maintain order.

The Indian government responded with a series of counterinsurgency measures, including the deployment of paramilitary forces and special police units.

The government also launched development programs aimed at addressing the underlying grievances of the tribal communities. However, these measures were largely ineffective, as they failed to address the root causes of the insurgency and often resulted in human rights abuses and the displacement of local populations.

The situation in Dantewada continued to deteriorate, with the Naxals launching more frequent and deadly attacks on government forces and installations. The government responded with greater force, leading to a cycle of violence and counter - violence that continues to this day.

Despite these efforts, the situation in Dantewada remains volatile. The Naxalites continue to launch deadly attacks on government forces and installations, while the government's counterinsurgency measures have led to human rights abuses and the displacement of local populations. The cycle of violence and counter-violence shows no signs of abating, and the people of Dantewada continue to live in fear and uncertainty.

Soon, the lovely land of Dantewada, which once upon a time was a peaceful place to live life and enjoy it, was converted into military base camps, and a lot of movement started happening. Naxal attacks on government offices and politicians have become very common. There was hardly a month when we didn't hear something new like this.

We learned one day that there had been an attack on politicians from our location. The whole family was traveling by car to someplace when the Naxals used their gorilla methodology to plant the bomb on the road. As soon as the car stepped on it, the blast happened, and the car was thrown some meters away from the spot. There were several rounds of firing using AK-47s at all the people sitting in the car. It was big news in the newspaper, and everyone in town was talking about it. My dad came home and asked me the name of Noor's father. As soon as I told them the name, my dad told me this was her family that was involved in this accident. He also told me that there were kids also in the car, and no one survived after this accident. The dead bodies were also taken by the Naxals and thrown in front of the local police station.

I was devastated as soon as I heard the story. Losing someone is not good, but this way, it was nothing less than a traumatic experience. It was not easy for me to cope with the thought that this has happened and I'll never be able to see Noor again. I didn't have enough courage to say a word. All I did was go numb. I stayed numb for almost a month. I haven't come out of the house and haven't even gone to school. It took me a lot of time to digest the fact that my Noor was no more. My parents tried to console me, but it was not easy for me to accept this.

After a month, I went back to school. I didn't find Noor in the class. It was all sad and empty for me. I looked at her bench, which was still empty. I also went to all the places where we used to spend time together, but I haven't found her anymore. I was getting mad inside, and I wanted to shout. I wanted to run away from all this to a place where I could no longer remember her.

I wanted to run away to a place where I could find no trace of her memory. I realized that if I stay longer in this place, I'll lose my balance and go mad.

I asked my parents about leaving this town. My parents initially resisted but eventually agreed for me to leave the place. I moved from Dantewada to Indore. I was admitted to a school here and started studying commerce. I did my bachelor's in commerce in Pune and then moved to the US to do my master's. I got a job at American Express as an investment banker. I spent the day in and day out working and have gained a lot of experience, made many contacts, and have a few very successful projects under my belt. I moved back to India and started my own firm to start investing in startups. I met Sneha at one of the startups I invested in. She reminded me of Noor at first, and that's how I grew interested in her. We eventually married up, and here I am sitting with you all, discussing my story.

"What a story you had!" said Ankit after a long pause. "Do you still miss her?" he asked.

"Yes. I do," said Nikhil, and he chose to get up from his place and walk to a corner in silence. No one else interrupted him, and everyone else focused on refilling their own glasses. Nikhil joined them after a while, and now all eyes are on Ankit.

Chapter 5
The Broken Love

After Nikhil finished this heart-touching story, a deep silence fell over the group. No one wanted to break it, but instead, they gave it some time to settle. Ankit was lost in deep thought as everyone started looking at him.

Ankit, after a short pause, took a deep breath and started. He started by confessing that his story is not as deep as Nikhil's. In the meantime, Nikhil also joined the group. He took his seat and started sipping his wine. He then, with a smile on his face, asked Ankit to start.

Nikhil started at the location where it all began. He said he was in Mumbai as a kid, and as per him, Mumbai is altogether a different world. The iconic landmark is the India Gate, a popular tourist spot, or let it be the Taj Mahal Hotel, which is the epitome of ultimate luxury. We have Juhu Beach with street food vendors, musicians, and tourists all vying for attention, and Marine Drive, a stretch of road along the coast of Mumbai, is a popular hangout spot for locals and tourists alike. This is a place where the rich and poor both find their hangout spots to live and enjoy. From Crawford Market to the most luxurious brand outlet, you have everything in Mumbai. This is a city where people hardly sleep, and this town definitely never sleeps.

I was also born and brought up in Andheri. It is a bustling neighborhood that is home to a diverse mix of people, including many middle-class families. The streets are lined with shops, markets, and restaurants, and there is always a sense of energy and activity in the air.

One of the most popular markets in Andheri is the Lokhandwala Market. It is a vibrant and bustling market that is always crowded with people. Here, you can find everything from clothes and accessories to fresh fruits and vegetables, spices, and home appliances. The vibrant and bustling Lokhandwala Market surrounds you with a cacophony of smells and sounds, as small street food stalls and eateries line the streets. The sizzle of frying pakoras mingles with the aroma of freshly brewed chai, enticing locals to stop for a quick snack or a sip of the steaming beverage. Brightly colored umbrellas provide shade from the sun, while the colorful displays of fresh fruits and vegetables beckon passersby to stop and peruse the wares.

Amidst the crowds and noise, it's easy to get swept up in the energy of the market and feel a sense of connection to the community. As you walk around the streets, you will see many small apartment buildings, each with its own unique character.

Many of these buildings have small shops or businesses on the ground floor, adding to the vibrant and bustling atmosphere of the area. I lived in a small complex called Purple Meadows on one of the streets here.

The people who lived in this complex are a mix of different cultures and backgrounds, but they all share a strong sense of community. You will see families out for walks or sitting on benches in the parks, children playing on the streets, and neighbors chatting over cups of tea. The streets are always busy, and there is a constant buzz of activity in the air.

Childhood in this locale is a vibrant and diverse experience. Walking down the streets, you might hear the lilting melody of Marathi mixed with the staccato rhythms of Hindi, as people from all over India and beyond go about their day. Children play games with friends from different backgrounds, swapping stories and sharing snacks, learning about the world around them, and gaining new perspectives. From the mouthwatering aromas of South Indian dosas to the glittering lights of a Diwali celebration, the diversity here infuses every aspect of daily life, creating a dynamic and rich environment for children to grow up in. The streets are always bustling with activity, and there is never a shortage of things to see and do.

One of the highlights of childhood in Andheri is the many parks and playgrounds in the area. Children can often be seen running around, playing games with friends, or taking part in organized sports activities. These green spaces provide a much - needed break from the busy streets and allow children to connect with nature and each other.

Another important part of childhood here is education. The neighborhood is home to a number of well - regarded schools, both public and private. Education is at the heart of most of the children living here. Kids spend countless hours studying and exploring the world around them, whether in the classroom or out on the streets. With a wealth of top-rated schools and a strong emphasis on academic success, the community fosters a love of learning that extends far beyond the classroom. Parents work tirelessly to support their children's education, attending parent - teacher meetings and volunteering at school events. As a result, children in Andheri grow up with a deep appreciation for the power of knowledge and a drive to succeed, no matter what challenges they may face.

I, too, was no different. Living in this part of Mumbai and the openness of my family helped shape my own open-mindedness. As a kid, I was known for my resilience and adaptability. We learned to navigate the complexities of the city from a young age and often formed close bonds with other children in the community. Communication and culture came to me naturally without having to put any effort into integrating myself and becoming street - smart.

I belong to a Gujarati business family that migrated to Mumbai generations ago to set up the business. The Gujrati business community is always a small, closed circle where everyone helps each other settle down.

Some generations ago, my grandparents, too, with the help of the community, ran a successful electronics showroom in Andheri. My father takes care of the business, and my mom is a house maker. They value education and hard work, and the children would likely be enrolled in some of the best schools in the city. The family would also place a high emphasis on traditions and customs, including food, music, and festivals.

In their free time, the family may be involved in community events and organizations, attend social gatherings, and network with other business leaders. They may also be active in philanthropic endeavors, giving back to the community through charitable donations and volunteer work. I saw Iit at one such event when I was almost fourteen years old. I was volunteering at the event. Most of the time, Gujrati's parents want their kids to volunteer at such events so that they get introduced to others in the community and also as a token of learning gratitude and value for every piece of work.

The hall was bustling with a lot of movement and commotion. Everyone was rushing around, organizing items, and setting up displays or equipment. We were busy creating a sense of energy and urgency in the setting and showing that we are highly motivated and driven to achieve our goals. Among this busy schedule and the hustle to show me busy it was then that I spotted Iti, a fellow volunteer who had caught my eye from the moment I had seen her profile on the organization's website.

She was busy setting up tables, moving boxes, and directing other volunteers with a smile on her face. I walked over to her and introduced myself, and she greeted me warmly, her eyes shining with kindness and a hint of mischief.

As the day wore on, I started finding ways to work side by side with her. I took on all the tasks that she was supervising.

In no time, we started sharing all the tasks together, sharing laughs, and trading smiles. I definitely wanted to leave a sense of connection in her mind so that she too could have the same feeling as I do. It was also on my mind to at least share phone numbers before we closed this event. I definitely wanted to see her again.

It was a typical Monday morning, and I was dragging myself to school as usual. Although I was good at studying, I still hated Mondays, especially since it meant I had to face my least favorite subject. Math. As I trudged through the school gates, I noticed a new face among the sea of students. It was a girl, with long, curly hair and a bright smile that lit up her face. I couldn't help but stare at her. All of a sudden, a smile covered my face. It didn't take me ages to identify that the girl is Iti. I was confused as the school dress that she was wearing is from some other school, and I also never saw her at this school.

I went to her and asked her, "Have you recognized me?" "Hey, Ankit. It's you." She said.

"What are you doing here?" I asked.

"We have an inter-school debate competition today, and I am here to represent my school," said Iti.

"Wow, debate competition." "I am sure others will have to look for ways to run away." "All the best," I said. I also remind her that she already has my phone number and can call me in case she needs any help at school.

I didn't want to sound very desperate, so I excused myself from there. Iti also smiled, said something, and carried on.

I rushed to a place to hide and kept noticing her from a distance, ensuring that she was not able to see me. All of a sudden, I started liking Mondays. It was for sure for two reasons. One, there is no math class today due to a debate competition, and second, the most obvious one is that we have Iti in my school. I am sure I'll not stop smiling the whole day.

All of a sudden, I rushed to my culture head and wanted to convince her that I was ready to participate in the debate competition. She said a big no to it because we already have our team representing the school. I was disappointed, but I showed my enthusiasm for her. She was somehow convinced that I could be included, but since there is no place for me to enter, she has to let me down.

I was sad to hear about her, but I was not discouraged. I started looking for ways to see who was representing our school in this event. I got the list from the staff room, and I have seen that Aman and Naveen are representing us. I knew both of them were solid contenders and that it would be great if they represented our school. Our chance to win the trophy will increase for sure. But then, all of a sudden, I thought that at the moment, the most important thing was for me to participate, not win the trophy. I started looking for ways to be included in this competition.

I looked at the watch, and it was just 30 minutes until the event started. I was standing there confused and praying to God to give me some magical insight to be able to participate in the event. The clock was ticking, and I was running out of ideas. I started sweating and growing more and more nervous.

Suddenly, I had a glow on my face when I saw Aman entering the washroom for a short urinal break. I followed him inside, and as soon as he entered the toilet, I locked the door from outside and put a magical board outside that read, "Defective, please use another facility."

I was excited as soon as I had done this. I also ensured that no one had seen me doing this. I went and started walking in and around the culture teacher. I could see the stress on her face when she was not seeing Aman anywhere. Naveen reached there, but without Aman, the chance to enter the competition will be gone. This is a pairs-only competition.

I went to the teacher and asked her if she needed any help. She told me that Aman is nowhere to be seen and that the time is ticking. I offered my services to run around and see if I could find him. I started running everywhere and returned without any luck. The teacher was worried, and then I offered to replace Aman just in case. Lacking any other options, Aman was out, and I was in. I was excited and thankful to God that the effort I put in had worked and I had gotten the result. I almost jumped with joy but had to control my happiness in front of the teacher. We all rushed towards the auditorium, and the competition began.

As I walked into the school auditorium, I saw her sitting in the front row, looking as beautiful as ever. My heart skipped a beat, and I felt my palms begin to sweat. The competition began, and everyone stepped into the auditorium for an introduction. We all shook hands and then stepped towards the dice to pick the topics. We had a political discussion, and we all went to our respective schools' seats, and the debate started.

The debate was intense, and everyone gave it their best shot. I noticed that I was becoming more and more conscious of her presence. Every time I looked at her, my mind would go blank, and I would forget my arguments.

Finally, it was my turn to speak, and I took a deep breath to calm my nerves. As I began to make my case, I saw her nodding in agreement, and it gave me the confidence to push on. I spoke with passion and conviction, pouring my heart into every word. The enthusiasm I received from seeing her boosted my performance. I did really well. I too shared the same enthusiasm when it was her time. She, too, did well.

When the debate ended, I approached her. We stepped out of the debate hall and found a quiet spot to continue their conversation. Ankit was eager to delve deeper into the topic they had debated, but he soon realized that his desire to keep the conversation going extended far beyond the subject at hand.

As we discussed the topic, I discovered that Iti possessed an impressive depth of knowledge and a genuine passion for the subject. Her insights and perspectives resonated with mine, and I found myself hanging on to every word she uttered. Time seemed to melt away as they engaged in a spirited exchange of ideas, their voices blending harmoniously amidst the backdrop of the bustling city.

Hours passed like fleeting moments, and we found ourselves laughing, sharing personal stories, and revealing our dreams and aspirations. The conversation effortlessly flowed, and we discovered shared interests and values that formed an unspoken bond between them. With each passing moment, my initial infatuation transformed into a profound connection-an undeniable sense that they were kindred spirits.

As the day drew to a close, the sun painted the sky with hues of orange and pink. I felt a mixture of excitement and longing, realizing that I had found someone truly special. I bid farewell to Iti, knowing deep down that this encounter was just the beginning of something extraordinary. We exchanged contact information, promising to keep in touch, and parted ways, our hearts buoyed with anticipation.

In the following days, our connection only grew stronger. We exchanged messages, eagerly continuing our conversations and discovering new facets of each other's personalities. Our exchanges became a delightful routine, woven into the fabric of our daily lives.

Weeks turned into months, and our bond flourished. We began spending more time together, exploring the vibrant streets of Mumbai, visiting art exhibitions, and indulging in our shared love for literature and cinema. Our friendship evolved into a beautiful romance-a story interlaced with stolen glances, gentle touchcs, and heartfelt confessions.

I marveled at Iti's vibrant Gujarati heritage, embracing the rich culture and traditions that she so passionately shared with him. I delighted in her stories of colorful festivals, mouthwatering delicacies, and the warmth of a close-knit community. Iti, in turn, cherished my unwavering support, my genuine interest in her dreams, and his ability to make her laugh even on the darkest days.

Together, we navigated the complexities of life, celebrating each other's triumphs and providing solace during challenging times. Our love was an anchor, grounding us amidst the swirling currents of the world around us.

As the months passed, our relationship continued to blossom. Our love became a steadfast presence, intertwined with their dreams, goals, and shared future. We embarked on countless adventures; our love story was intertwined with the vibrant tapestry of Mumbai-a city that bore witness to their journey and played an integral part in shaping our lives like a million others.

This continued well until we were in our final years of school. But then we found ourselves facing a new kind of confusion that began to creep into their love lives, casting shadows of doubt and testing the strength of our bond. It all started when the pressure of approaching exams and the impending transition to different colleges began to take their toll on us.

As our focus shifted towards our individual futures, the once unbreakable connection they had built together started to feel strained. I became preoccupied with my studies, spending long hours buried in books and losing touch with the vibrant conversations and shared moments that had defined their relationship. Iti, too, became engulfed in her own worries and aspirations, grappling with the overwhelming demands of academics and the uncertainties that lay ahead.

It generally happens. When we are too much into studies and careers, we tend to start dwelling more in the imagination of the future than in the present. We start dreaming of achieving a future and tend to forget that we also have a present, and it's more important to live and cherish that. We become so futuristic that presents start irritating us, and we tend to find solace in books or somewhere else.

Emotions ran high as the insidious tendrils of confusion crept gradually and relentlessly into our lives. Amidst the ceaseless whirlwind of responsibilities and towering expectations, our once harmonious interactions began to bear the weight of misunderstandings and miscommunications. With each passing day, our time together grew scarce, leaving us yearning for those precious moments that seemed to slip through our fingers. The absence of cherished shared experiences and meaningful connections took a heavy toll on our once vibrant emotional bond, leaving us feeling hollow, distant, and painfully disconnected.

In our attempt to juggle our personal aspirations with the demands of our relationship, we found ourselves questioning the compatibility of our dreams and ambitions. Doubts about our future together and the sacrifices required began to chip away at the foundation of trust we had painstakingly built.

Caught in the throes of confusion, we started second - guessing our feelings and our ability to navigate the challenges that lay ahead. Fear and insecurity crept in, clouding our judgment and overshadowing the love we had once shared so deeply.

Conversations that were once filled with laughter and understanding turned into tense discussions and arguments. The emotional toll became evident as trust wavered, and we found ourselves questioning whether they could truly support each other's individual growth while maintaining the connection we cherished.

Gradually, the weight of the confusion became too heavy to bear, and we found ourselves at a crossroads. The toll on our love and trust had become too great, and we could no longer ignore the growing doubts that plagued our hearts.

With heavy hearts and tear-filled eyes, we made the painful decision to take a break and explore life's uncertainties individually. We hoped that some time and space apart would provide clarity and help us understand what we truly wanted from our lives and our relationship.

During our time apart, we underwent a period of self-reflection and introspection. We realized that the confusion we had experienced stemmed from the immense pressure we had put on ourselves and the fear of losing our individual identities in the pursuit of love. It became clear that we needed to find a balance between our personal aspirations and the commitment we had to each other.

Sometimes I remember how our hearts used to beat in sync, our laughter filled the air, and our dreams intertwined like the threads of a delicate tapestry. We were inseparable, finding solace in each other's presence and drawing strength from our shared aspirations, and today we want to part because of everything that we liked about each other. Time plays really well and shows us unique experiences every time.

The weight of responsibilities and the burden of towering expectations began to cast a shadow on our once vibrant love. I decided to escape this and have made a bold decision. I enrolled in a bachelor's program and embarked on a journey to America, hoping to find solace and a fresh start. I studied hard and cleared all the exams, which enabled me to take this leap in my career. My parents, too, were happy with the decisions and have supported my move. Without telling or discussing this with Iti, I decided to do all this on my own and move on without her.

I reached America and started my fall. New place, new people, and no one who can remind me of my past. With all this, I immersed myself in my studies, trying to drown out the echoes of the memories that haunted me. I discovered new passions and explored different horizons, hoping to find a sense of purpose in my newfound surroundings. Although physically distant from my past, my heart still carried the weight of the love he once shared with Iti.

It's never easy to forget or forgo your first love. Every new girl I met, I tried to find Iti in her, and hence I never again had any other relations. This helped me stay focused on my studies and research on the topics I always wanted to focus on. Global economics became my newfound love suddenly, and I found myself soon immersed in this. There will be no book left that I have not read on the topic. I managed to establish myself as an expert on the subject at my university.

Meanwhile, Iti found herself caught up in the whirlwind of social media. As she embraced the digital realm, her charisma and captivating personality attracted a massive following. She became a celebrity social media influencer and her every move was scrutinized by adoring fans. The superficial world of likes and followers provided a temporary respite from the void in her heart.

I too followed her on all the possible social media platforms so that I could keep getting updates on her whereabouts. I once dared to message her on one of the platforms, but I never received any response. This left me broke, and I kept thinking that maybe we are too busy now to even respond.

Sometimes, life takes unexpected turns, and the paths we once thought would intertwine forever end up leading us in different directions. Such was our case too, with two souls whose love story had once burned brightly but now existed only as a bittersweet memory.

Their lives took divergent paths, carrying us to distant corners of the world. I found myself drawn to the fast-paced world of finance, pursuing a career as an investment banker with Goldman Sachs. The demanding nature of my profession consumed my time and energy, leaving little room for anything else.

Iti, on the other hand, found success in the world of ad films. Her talent and charisma shone brightly on the silver screen, captivating audiences across the country. With each film, she climbed higher on the ladder of fame, becoming a sensational hit in India. The spotlight embraced her, but deep down, she carried the fragments of a love story left untold.

As the years passed, we occasionally caught glimpses of each other's lives through social media and news articles. I followed Iti's rise to stardom from afar, a mixture of pride and longing tugging at my heart. Iti, too, found herself searching for traces of my presence in the digital realm, wondering what could have been.

Despite our successes and the lives we had built independently, both of us carried a lingering sense of unfinished business. Their hearts still held a space for each other, a space filled with the memories of what once was and the unspoken words left unsaid.

In the depths of my office, surrounded by the bustling world of finance, I often found myself reminiscing about the days when Iti's laughter filled the air. The ache in my heart grew with each passing day, a longing for the connection we had lost. The glamour and wealth that accompanied my success as an investment banker felt hollow in comparison to the depth and purity of the love I had once known.

As fate would have it, a few months later, when the demands of their respective careers had settled, we found ourselves in the same city once again. The universe seemed to conspire to bring them together, offering a glimmer of hope that perhaps their paths would cross and their unfinished story could find its conclusion.

But life had other plans. My demanding schedule as an investment banker left me with little free time. It's commitments in the film industry were equally relentless, with shooting schedules and promotional events monopolizing her days. Our paths, though seemingly close, remained parallel and never converged.

We once planned to catch up through social media messages, and she responded too. We decided to meet in a restaurant, but unfortunately, Iti didn't turn up as she was busy with some promotions about the new movie she is in. I kept waiting in the restaurant forever for her to come, and later I heard in the news that she was busy promoting her movie. I understood that this event was more important for her, and she chose to attend it.

And so, despite the lingering love that echoed in their hearts, we moved forward separately, each finding success and fulfillment in our chosen paths. We carried the memories of their time together as a cherished treasure, a reminder of a love that had once burned passionately but had been dimmed by the passage of time and the choices we had made.

I thrived in my career, making significant contributions to the world of finance and amassing wealth along the way. Iti continued to shine on the silver screen, captivating audiences with her talent and beauty. Both achieved remarkable success in our respective fields, becoming symbols of determination and accomplishment.

But success and fame could never fill the void that existed in our hearts. Despite our achievements, there remained a part of us that yearned for the connection we had lost-the depth of understanding, the shared dreams, and the unwavering support that only we could offer each other.

After years of carrying the weight of unfulfilled love, I made a life-altering decision. I chose to pursue the rest of my career in India. This has already become the place to be and build a career. Also, my heart yearns for a fresh start. With newfound determination, I embarked on a journey to rediscover myself and embrace the possibilities that lay ahead.

It was during one of my client meetings that fate intervened, introducing me to Riya. As we exchanged pleasantries and engaged in casual conversation, a spark ignited between us. Riya's infectious laughter and genuine warmth resonated with me, reminding him of the joy I had once known. Our connection blossomed effortlessly, and what started as friendship soon blossomed into a deep and meaningful mature relationship.

Our trust and bond started growing stronger with each passing day. We explored the depths of each other's souls, sharing dreams, fears, and aspirations. Riya's presence brought a renewed sense of happiness and purpose to my life, slowly mending the fragments of his heart that had long been dormant.

As we navigated the joys and challenges of our relationship, we recognized the importance of building a foundation of trust and understanding. We cherished the moments we spent together, creating beautiful memories that overshadowed the remnants of the past. I found solace in Riya's unwavering support and her ability to see beyond the scars I carried.

After a year of dating, we knew that we had found something extraordinary. Our love had weathered the storms of uncertainty and emerged stronger than ever. We decided to take the next step in their journey together and commit to a lifetime of love and companionship.

With our families' blessings and the love and support of their friends, we embarked on the beautiful journey of marriage. Our wedding day was a celebration of love, filled with laughter, tears of joy, and the promise of a future intertwined.

As we stood together, hand in hand, exchanging vows and promises, I couldn't help but feel a sense of closure. The pain and longing that had once consumed his heart were replaced with a profound gratitude for the journey that led him to Riya. In her eyes, I saw the reflection of a love that was destined to be, a love that had finally found its rightful place in his life.

Our union was not just a mere blending of two lives; it was a collision of dreams, hopes, and aspirations that illuminated their path forward. The world seemed to come alive with vibrant hues, as if nature itself rejoiced in their love story. Every sunrise held the promise of a new beginning, and every sunset whispered a lullaby of serenity and contentment.

With Riya by my side, I discovered a profound sense of purpose and completeness. Her presence ignited a fire within me, igniting a passion for life that I had never experienced before. Our love was an anchor, a sanctuary amidst the chaos of the world. In Riya's embrace, I found solace-a safe haven where he could lay bare his vulnerabilities and be embraced with unconditional love. Her gentle touch had the power to heal wounds, mend broken spirits, and breathe life into his weary soul.

As we traversed the labyrinth of life, we discovered that marriage was not just a mere contract but a profound commitment to nurturing and growing together. We embarked on adventures, big and small, creating memories that would forever be etched in the tapestry of their lives. From spontaneous road trips to quiet evenings spent stargazing, we reveled in the simple joys that love bestowed upon us.

Marriage bestows upon us the gift of growth and transformation. We learned the art of compromise, the beauty of selflessness, and thc joy of shared dreams. In each other's eyes, we saw the reflection of our dreams, and we vowed to walk hand in hand, supporting and uplifting each other through every triumph and tribulation.

And so, as we continued to write the chapters of our love story, we embraced the unknown, knowing that as long as we had each other, we had everything we needed. With love as our compass and our hearts intertwined, we set forth, ready to face the ever-unfolding tapestry of life, hand in hand, forever bound by a love that would withstand the test of time.

Wow, amazing, said Rohan.

And you guys are doing great still. I liked the story. But do you know what has happened to it? Asked Rohan Again.

Once I met Riya, I stopped following her up and got busy with my own life, said Ankit. Maybe better would be to search for her on Instagram, and you would know, He added further.

Everybody laughed around and started looking at Rishi to start his story.

Chapter 6
A Journey of Passion And Transformation

It all started in a small district of Uttarakhand called Chamoli. We used to have our ancestral property in a village called Auli. This place offers a mesmerizing panorama of snow-capped mountains, lush green meadows, and dense coniferous forests. The village is particularly famous for its stunning ski slopes, which attract adventure enthusiasts and nature lovers from around the world. During the winter months, the entire landscape transforms into a winter wonderland with powdery snow, making Auli one of the finest ski destinations in India.

In addition to its allure for adventure sports, Auli captivates visitors with its serene and idyllic atmosphere. The air is crisp and refreshing, allowing you to escape the hustle and bustle of city life. As you explore the village, you'll be enchanted by the picturesque vistas at every turn.

One of the highlights of Auli is the panoramic view it offers of some of the highest peaks in the Himalayas, including Nanda Devi, Mana Parvat, and Kamet. The sunrise and sunset views from Auli are truly awe - inspiring, painting the sky with vibrant hues that reflect off the snow - clad mountains.

The village is also blessed with vibrant flora and fauna. During spring and summer, the meadows are adorned with a carpet of colorful wildflowers, creating a magical sight. Auli's beauty is not limited to any specific season, as each season brings its own charm and allure.

If you seek tranquility, Auli provides ample opportunities for leisurely walks, meditation, and reconnecting with nature. You can also indulge in local cuisine and warm hospitality, immersing yourself in the local culture.

A visit to Auli is a journey into a world of untouched natural splendor, where the magnificence of the Himalayas will leave you awe - inspired and rejuvenated. We also had a small property where we allowed tourists to stay when we were not there. We had a property manager who used to take care of everything in our absence.

We once visited here when I was in my youth, maybe when I was 16 or 17 years old. Everything is different during this period. The strange feeling of attraction towards every other sex is very natural, and the desire to lure everyone was newly budding in me. The feeling of attraction or desire towards women during youth is natural. This feeling is often referred to as "youthful infatuation" or "young love." These emotions can be strong and intense as individuals explore their emerging sexuality and navigate their relationships with others.

During this trip, I happened to meet Sangeeta at my house. She was a distant relative of our caretaker. She was very beautiful, and her look captured my attention. She was also of my age. I was glued to her as soon as I saw her. Her beauty was unparalleled, and her captivating presence attracted the attention of many suitors.

The first time Sangeeta laid eyes on me, her breath caught in her throat, and her heart skipped a beat. My piercing blue eyes met hers with an intensity that sent shivers down her spine. In that fleeting moment, time seemed to stand still as their gazes locked, and the world around us faded into insignificance.

Sangeeta possessed a beauty that was enchanting and ethereal, captivating all who crossed her path. Her physical features were a symphony of elegance and grace. Silken strands of chestnut hair cascaded down her shoulders, framing a face that seemed to have been carved by the hands of angels. Her eyes were like deep pools of mystery, sparkling with a mixture of curiosity and warmth. They held the power to draw people in, revealing a soul that was both gentle and fiercely passionate.

Her smile was a radiant sunbeam, capable of lighting up the darkest of rooms. It was a smile that seemed to carry a secret-a tantalizing invitation to explore the depths of her soul. Her lips, soft and inviting, held the promise of whispered words of love and tender kisses.

Sangeeta's slender figure moved with a natural grace, as if she were effortlessly gliding through life. Her poise was a testament to her inner strength and confidence, creating an aura of magnetic charm that left an indelible impression on those fortunate enough to cross her path.

As people interact with Sangeeta, they may experience a range of emotions. Her genuine interest in their stories and her ability to listen without judgment create a safe space for vulnerability. They may feel seen and understood, as if they have found a kindred spirit who truly cares.

I was truly attracted to her, and I wanted to know her more. In my rush to know her more, I went to her and introduced myself to her.

"Hi, I am Rishi. I am the son of this property owner. We are here to spend my summer vacation." I introduced myself.

"Hello, I am Sangeeta. I am the relative of your property's caretaker. I come here often to spend some time in this serene place. I stay in Dehradun, but I like to visit here. I stay with my uncle here every time I come here." She responded back.

"So you are not a stranger to this place. Can you please show me this place? Although we have property here and we visit here sometimes, I still feel like I am a stranger to this place." I said.

Sangeeta gladly agreed to take me to the various places. Our parents also had no problem with this arrangement, as we were staying in the same place. We trust Sangeeta's uncle a lot, and we have known him for a long time now. There is no reason for us to doubt him or any of his relatives. So here we go. I had a chance to spend a lot of time with her.

I was excited, and the youth in me was telling me that this was the chance I was waiting for. I was excited to see how this would develop, but in my mind, I already imagined Sangeeta and I kissing and hugging each other, Singing romantic songs, like in Hindi movies, and beginning a new chapter in life. See, as a youth, even I was very much inspired by the shit shows shown in Hindi movies.

Sangeeta's beauty was not just skin-deep; it emanated from within, shining through in every word she spoke and every gesture she made. Her presence was a breath of fresh air, a beacon of light in a world often overshadowed by darkness. She had the rare ability to make others feel seen, heard, and loved, leaving an indelible mark on their souls.

In the end, it was the combination of Sangeeta's outward grace and inner radiance that made her beauty truly unforgettable. It was a beauty that went beyond the surface, a beauty that encompassed both her physical features and the depth of her character. Sangeeta was a living testament to the fact that true beauty lies not just in appearance but in the way one embraces life and touches the hearts of others.

The next morning, she met me at the breakfast table to take me to Places. She was wearing a light yellow top with blue jeans. I was stuck in breezy fabrics that gently caressed her skin, allowing her to move with ease and radiate a natural glow. She often opts for pastel shades and soft hues, reminiscent of the gentle colors of a blossoming sunrise.

Her outfits are characterized by their minimalistic yet stylish designs. She embraces clean lines and subtle details, favoring classic silhouettes that accentuate her natural beauty. Her ensembles are a testament to the adage that less is more, as she effortlessly captures attention through her understated elegance.

Accessorizing with a discerning eye, she carefully selects delicate pieces that add a touch of charm to her overall look. Perhaps it's a dainty pendant necklace that gracefully rests upon her collarbone or a simple bracelet adorning her wrist; each accessory serves to enhance her natural radiance rather than overpower it. My eyes were glued to her.

She reached out to me and asked me to finish the breakfast soon. She warned me of the long day we would have. I finished the breakfast in haste, and I was ready for the day of my life to begin. It felt like this was the moment I was alive. I will not complain, even if this is the last day of my life.

We started, and it was a great feeling to have her by my side. I also observed a lot of people staring at me. I was sure they were jealous of me and were cursing me in their heads.

I, too, was not bad at looking. I was a striking figure, possessing a magnetic presence that commanded attention. Tall and lean, I carried myself with an effortless confidence that hinted at a depth of character. My dark, tousled hair framed a face adorned with rugged features, giving me an air of both mystery and rugged charm. In short, we were certainly looking like we were made for each other, and we were looking great together.

Our eyes collided many times during the day. I am sure my eyes held a captivating allure, drawing Sangeeta into their depths. They seemed to hold a thousand stories, whispered secrets, and untold adventures. In their cerulean depths, she glimpsed a potent mix of both strength and vulnerability, as if he were a complex tapestry of emotions waiting to be unraveled.

His smile was a blend of mischief and genuine warmth, revealing a set of perfectly sculpted lips that could effortlessly convey tenderness and passion. There was an undeniable magnetism in his presence, an energy that tugged at her very core, awakening a desire she had never felt before.

We couldn't help but feel a surge of curiosity and intrigue, as if an invisible thread had connected our souls in that momentary encounter. Her mere presence stirred a sense of excitement and anticipation within her, leaving me yearning to discover more about the spark within her.

We visited many places together, and she was so passionate about showing me the places. She also took me to a very quiet and lonely place where we sat for hours without uttering a word but still enjoying ourselves. We were watching the sunset together with no one to disturb us. The whole moment was ours, and it felt as if the sun was setting exclusively for us that day. It felt as if time had stopped and this moment would never end. The sweet fragrance of her perfume was pulling me more towards her and making my mind foggy.

Sitting over here, I touched her hands, and she didn't resist. It felt so nice to have her hand in mine. I was feeling as if I were the owner of the universe and that the entire universe was in my hands. I never wanted this moment to go, and I wanted to live in this moment forever. I can feel similar emotions reaching out to me from her side too.

I noticed a strange sense of a combination of physical sensations, emotional connection, and a heightened sense of vulnerability. Very soon, we found ourselves exploring and discovering each other's bodies, desires, and boundaries in a safe and consensual manner. Our hands were vigorously moving over each other's bodies. We hugged each other so tightly and stayed like that for some time.

We felt a mix of nervousness, excitement, and anticipation. All of a sudden, we realized the growing bond between us. In the moment of attraction, we felt that time seemed to slow down and that the world around us had faded away. Suddenly we realized that our lips had collided, and the first touch of lips was so gentle and tentative. We both explored and navigated this new level of intimacy. It was a soft and lingering kiss, filled with warmth and tenderness. It has ignited a spark of passion and intensity, and the chemistry between us has started to deepen.

All of a sudden, we realized that we had just met the day before and were so closely bonded that day. We gained consciousness and linked ourselves back to our surroundings. We came back to the moment, and all I heard from Sangeeta was that we should head back to the villa as it was already too late. I just followed the instructions coming from her and have followed her. We uttered no more words at that moment. We reached the villa and parted for our own rooms. What a day it was. I was excited as well as astonished.

I slept on my bed that night, cherishing the memory and the emotions associated with that first kiss we just had. I can still feel the softness of her lips, and I can feel her with me. I was thinking that this day has served as a special milestone in our relationship, fostering a deeper connection and setting the stage for further romantic exploration together.

This forbidden encounter became a secret dance of temptation. We couldn't resist the allure of each other's company; our hearts pounded with anticipation every time we met. I was not sure from my end whether this was love or the attraction that this age brings to most of us. I always felt the longing and desire to be with her. I can see the lust within me, which was always pulling me towards her. I never felt this strong for anyone else before. I was more than sure that for Sangeeta, it was not the same. She yearned for something more profound-a connection that transcended mere physicality.

I realized that Sangeeta is here just for a week this time. She told me that she is on some assignment here for a week, and then she will move back to Dehradun. This is where she is currently staying and is looking forward to completing her bachelor's degree from some of the best colleges in Mumbai. She said she was good in her studies but probably could not continue much due to her family background. There was no breadwinner in her family, and she has to earn money on her own to continue her studies. She stays alone in Dehradun, too.

Amidst the flames of desire, we were sometimes plagued by doubts and uncertainties. We questioned whether our feelings were merely driven by physical attraction-a fleeting infatuation that would dissipate over time. The rapid intensity of the emotions left me questioning whether what I felt was true love or an illusion created by the intoxicating allure of lust.

Among all these confusions, Sangeeta embarked on a quest to unravel the complexities of the emotions and bonding between us. She engaged in deep conversations with me sometimes, seeking to understand my dreams, fears, and values. We shared moments of vulnerability and intimacy, delving beyond the surface and forging a connection that started to extend beyond the physical realm.

As we started spending time together and our relationship evolved, Sangeeta's confusion gradually subsided. She began to recognize that what she had initially mistaken for mere lust was, in fact, a seed of love taking root within our hearts. The intensity of our physical attraction remained, but it was now complemented by a growing emotional bond, a shared understanding, and a profound connection that transcended the boundaries of mere desire.

My journey from confusion to clarity was a transformative one for me too. It taught me that true love is not devoid of physical desire but rather a harmonious blend of both passion and deep emotional connection. In me, she found a partner who helped her navigate the tumultuous sea of emotions, guiding her toward a love that was built on a solid foundation of trust, understanding, and mutual respect.

We've started meeting every day now. In fact, every day I would just wait for her to be visible and continue to think about her being visible throughout the day. She sometimes takes a break for something else. She told me that she was here on an assignment, and whenever she was away, I would just wait for her to be back.

With each passing day, I started getting the feeling that our bonding was getting deeper and deeper. Our love burned like a flame, igniting with every stolen kiss and tender touch. Each encounter was a testament to our deep emotional connection, transcending the physical realm.

We decided to go for a walk after dinner. It was a bright evening, and the beauty of Auli has increased. It looked like the entire town had worn a white curtain, and everyone slept. It was so quiet and peaceful out there.

It was difficult to imagine this if you saw the tourist packed Auli in bright daylight. The cold breeze was adding fuel to the fire, and Sangeeta and I walking together, step by step, was a great rush of emotion and fulfillment for me.

In the moonlit embrace of our favorite park, our lips met, our mouths melding in a delicate dance of desire. Soft whispers of affection passed between us, as if our words were the gentle caress of a summer breeze. Our kisses were a symphony of longing, an exchange of love that conveyed more than words ever could.

We rushed to the villa and headed directly to my room. This was the first time we were together in my room when everyone else in the villa had already slept. We hugged each other so tightly as soon as the door was bolted from inside. As our bodies entwined, our encounters became a tapestry of sensations - skin against skin, hearts racing in synchrony. We reveled in the electric chemistry that bound us, exploring each other with reverence and tenderness. It was a dance of vulnerability and trust, guided by unspoken consent and a profound understanding of one another's desires.

Sangeeta's fingers traced the contours of my back, leaving a trail of tingling sensations in their wake. Our connection went beyond physical pleasure; it was an intimate exploration of our souls. Each touch was an expression of love, a testament to our deepening bond.

We sought solace in the subtleties; the language of our bodies spoke volumes. A stolen glance ignited a fire within us, and a single touch created a crescendo of passion. Our encounters were a symphony of desire, the melodies and harmonies orchestrated with care and respect.

After the encounter, we lay intertwined, our bodies glowing with a shared warmth. It was in these quiet moments, in the aftermath, that our love truly flourished. We basked in the serenity of their connection, our breaths intermingling as we reveled in the profound love we had discovered.

Wow, it sounded like poetry to my ears, said Arjun all of a sudden.

Rohan too added, I can just imagine the depth of love you had. I envy you, my friend. What a past! I am dying to hear the next part. Please continue.

As the gentle afterglow enveloped us in a warm embrace, Sangeeta nestled her head against my chest, feeling the steady rhythm of my heartbeat. Her voice trembled with a mixture of vulnerability and honesty as she mustered the courage to share her conflicted feelings.

"Rishi," she began, her words laced with both affection and apprehension, "I need to tell you something that has been weighing on my heart. I love you deeply, more than words can express. Our connection is something truly special, and you've brought immense joy into my life."

She paused, her fingertips tracing circles on my skin, the touch both comforting and uncertain. "But there's someone else. Someone who possesses the financial security that I find myself longing for. It's not an easy admission to make, and it hurts me to say this, but I feel torn between my heart and the practicalities of life."

My brows furrowed, a mix of confusion and sadness etching my face. I tightened my embrace, conveying a mixture of compassion and concern. "Sangeeta, I appreciate your honesty, but remember that love is not solely defined by material wealth. It's about the connection we share, the support we offer, and the dreams we can build together."

I gently brushed a stray strand of hair behind her ear. My voice was filled with tenderness. "I understand the complexities that life presents, but true love transcends material possessions. If we face challenges together, we can find our own path to happiness."

Sangeeta's eyes glistened with tears, a blend of conflicting emotions coursing through her. She met my gaze, her voice trembling but resolute. "I need to be honest with you. This was not an easy decision for me, either. I've decided to pursue a relationship with someone who possesses greater financial security. But I want you to know that it's not because I don't love you."

My eyes widened, and a mix of surprise and pain flashed across my face. I tried to speak, but the words caught in my throat. Sangeeta continued, her voice filled with regret: "I thought that wealth and security were what I needed, but I've come to realize that love, true love, can never be replaced by material possessions."

Tears welled up in her eyes as she reached out to touch my cheek. "You've shown me what it means to love and be loved unconditionally. Our connection is something rare and precious. I was blinded by the allure of wealth, but I now see that true happiness lies in the depth of our love and the memories we've shared."

Her gaze softened as he listened, his heart aching with the weight of her decision. "Sangeeta, I understand your need for security, but remember that love is not defined by financial status alone. It's about the journey we're willing to take together, supporting and growing with one another. If you ever realize that money can't replace what we have, I'll be here, waiting with open arms."

"I understand every word you are saying, and I know that you mean every word you are saying here. I am also feeling fortunate to have found you in my life. The decision is made, and I am leaving. I hope you will forgive me and move on with your life. You will not chase me and will never try to cross our path." Sangeeta said before she rushed out of the room. I was lying quietly in bed as if I had no sense. I only knew I was alive because the tears were not stopping from my eyes, and her words were echoing in my head constantly.

After Sangeeta left, my world crumbled around her. The pain of heartbreak weighed heavily on my shoulders, and I found myself immersed in a sea of sadness and confusion. For days, I felt lost and unable to make sense of the shattered pieces of our once beautiful relationship. My Family was a bit worried about me. They have noticed the sudden change in my behavior. I no longer wanted to be in Auli, especially in the Villa. Every room and every corner of the house reminds me of the moment I spent with Sangeeta. All of a sudden, the cool breeze, which was making this place heaven on earth, has gone suffocating.

The fact that she left me and my love for someone who has more money than I have is daunting to me. My heart sank, and a surge of emotions filled my being. The room suddenly felt suffocating as the weight of her words settled on him. I felt the sting of rejection and a deep sense of heartbreak, unable to comprehend how our love had been overshadowed by financial gain.

The cloud of confusion in my thoughts is simple. I was thinking, what about the love we shared? The plans we made together? How could she or someone prioritize money over us?

I was feeling the weight of betrayal, questioning my own worth and the authenticity of any relationship. The pain of this impending separation is palpable, as is the unraveling of their once unbreakable bond. With every passing hour, I found myself enveloped in a sea of heartbreak. My mind replayed memories of our love, trying to make sense of Sangeeta's choice.

We decided to leave Auli and move back to Indore. I was determined that I'd never be able to come back to this Auli, as every corner of this place reminds me of the time spent together with Sangeeta.

As the weight of heartbreak lingered, I knew he had to pick up the pieces of his life and find a way to move forward. Determined to create a secure future for myself, I harnessed my pain as fuel for self-improvement.

With unwavering determination, I dove into my studies, immersing myself in banking and finance as my area of expertise.

I sought solace in knowledge, burying myself in books, lectures, and hands-on experiences. The pursuit of academic excellence became my refuge, providing a sense of purpose and direction.

Every lecture, every assignment, and every exam became a stepping stone toward a brighter future. My focus was laser-sharp as I dedicated countless hours to my studies, my hunger for success intensifying with each passing day. I understood that building my knowledge and expertise would be the foundation for the financial security I sought.

Alongside his studies, I engaged in self-growth. I delved into personal development books, attended seminars, and sought mentorship from individuals who had achieved financial success. I cultivated a mindset of abundance, constantly reminding myself of the importance of financial stability to prevent being left behind.

The pain of past heartbreak fueled my desire to build wealth. I immersed myself in the intricacies of finance, investment strategies, and entrepreneurship. I saw every opportunity as a stepping stone toward my financial goals, driven by the belief that building wealth would safeguard my future relationships.

Months turned into years, and my hard work paid off. Armed with my knowledge, dedication, and unwavering focus, I navigated the world of business with confidence and skill. I seized opportunities, made wise investments, and built a successful career that surpassed my initial aspirations.

Amidst my achievements, I realized that true wealth extended beyond monetary gains. I focused on nurturing meaningful connections and creating a balanced life that encompassed not only financial stability but also love, joy, and personal fulfillment.

As I navigated through life's twists and turns, I encountered someone who sparked a deep connection and resonated with his newfound sense of self. This new person, Sophia, brought a fresh perspective into my life and shared his values, dreams, and aspirations.

Sophia was a kindred spirit who understood me in ways he had never experienced before. Our compatibility was evident, as we effortlessly complemented one another's strengths and weaknesses. With Sophia, I found a human being who supported my ambitions, celebrated his accomplishments, and stood by his side through every challenge.

Our relationship flourished as we nurtured a profound emotional bond built on trust, respect, and open communication. I felt a renewed sense of happiness and fulfillment in this partnership as we embarked on shared adventures, pursued common goals, and created a foundation of love and support.

My relationship with Sophia not only enriched my personal life but also inspired me to make a positive impact in the world. Together, we dedicated our time and resources to causes we deeply cared about, using our collective influence to create meaningful change. I found a sense of purpose and fulfillment in their shared commitment to making a difference. I also run a charitable organization with Sophie, and together we are happy to see life transform.

And Here I am today, with all of you, to explore my other passion. Watching the sunset in a silent corner, away from the hustle and bustle of city life. That's my life, and that's my reason to look forward to owning this garden so that I can spend some calm time with myself.

"And what about Sangeeta? Have you ever met her? Has she ever tried to contact you back?" asked Ankit.

It was a gentleman's promise before we parted that we would not follow or contact each other after the last evening, and I am following the promise I made to her. I never tried to reach back to her. Whenever I watch the sunset, that reminds me of the unconditional love I have received, and I keep thinking of the possible reasons why she left me. Also, I never went back to Auli after this.

Every one saw Rishi deeply imbued in silence, and they didn't want to disturb him, so they chose to sip the wine and conclude the night. They all went back to their rooms, leaving the fire in the fireplace turning to ashes as the night passed.

Conclusion

In the aftermath of a painful breakup, a broken heart found solace in resilience and determination. Fueled by the fire within, it channeled the pain into a relentless pursuit of personal growth and making a positive impact on the world.

With each shattered piece of the heart, a renewed sense of purpose emerged. The individual delved into self-reflection, exploring the depths of their emotions and uncovering hidden strengths. They embarked on a journey of healing and self-discovery, determined to transform their pain into something meaningful.

As the broken heart worked diligently to rebuild its shattered core, it harnessed newfound determination and redirected its energy towards effecting change. This journey of self-improvement inspired a powerful transformation that would not only shape the individual's life but also touch the lives of others.

We have seen one thing common in all the stories above. They all had breakups, and they all realized that there is life beyond love and breakups. You can gather courage to gather yourself and stand against all the odds, and all of them have achieved success beyond imagination.

Indeed, the common thread that weaves through the stories is the profound realization that there is life beyond love and breakups. Each protagonist discovered the strength within themselves to gather courage, stand tall against the odds, and forge a path towards success that surpassed their wildest dreams.

Breakups can be emotionally devastating, leaving one feeling lost, shattered, and uncertain about the future. However, these stories demonstrate that even in the midst of heartbreak, the human spirit possesses incredible resilience and the capacity for personal growth.

Through the pain and challenges they faced, the characters in these stories tapped into their inner reserves of strength and determination. They harnessed their experiences as catalysts for change, fueling their drive to overcome adversity and prove their worth to themselves and the world.

With unwavering courage, they faced their fears head-on and embraced the opportunities that came their way. They refused to let their past define them, and instead, they turned their pain into a powerful force for transformation. They channeled their emotions into productive pursuits, striving for success in their chosen fields.

As they persevered and pushed past their limitations, they achieved remarkable feats, exceeding their own expectations. Their stories serve as inspiration to others, demonstrating that even in the face of heartbreak, one can rise above the pain, reinvent themselves, and achieve extraordinary success.

These characters serve as living proof that the journey after a breakup can lead to unexpected and remarkable accomplishments. They discovered that love and relationships are important parts of life, but they are not the sole determinants of one's worth or happiness.

By focusing on personal growth, harnessing inner strength, and pursuing their passions, they found fulfillment and achieved success that surpassed their imagination. Their stories remind us that resilience, determination, and the willingness to embrace new opportunities can lead to incredible transformations and a life beyond what we once thought possible.

So, to anyone experiencing heartbreak, take heart from these stories and know that there is a world of possibilities awaiting you. Gather your courage, stand against the odds, and dare to create a future that surpasses your wildest dreams.

With each turn of the page, the love stories unfolded, painting a tapestry of shared experiences and heartfelt emotions. Through the highs and lows, the twists and turns, a profound sense of fulfillment took root within our hearts. We had journeyed together, navigating the intricacies of love, and emerged stronger and more deeply connected than we ever thought possible.

Love, with its inexplicable power, has woven its magic throughout our lives. It had touched our souls, transforming us in ways we could have never imagined. In the moments of joy, laughter, and shared dreams, we found solace and a deep sense of belonging. Love became the guiding force that illuminated our path, enveloping us in its warm embrace.

Through the challenges they faced, love served as our anchor, grounding us during the storms of life. It reminded us of the strength we possessed, individually and as a couple, urging us to persevere and find beauty even in the darkest of moments. Love was our guiding light, illuminating the way forward with hope and resilience.

We Show the transformative power of love. It challenged them to grow, to learn from their mistakes, and to become better versions of themselves. Love compelled us to confront our shortcomings, to communicate openly, and to prioritize the well-being of our shared journey.

As we neared the end of each love story, a tapestry of cherished memories and shared experiences unfolded. Their hearts overflowed with gratitude for the love they had found and the way it had shaped our lives. We were humbled by the depth of our connection and the profound impact love had on our souls.

As the final lines of each love story were written, we closed the chapter with a sense of fulfillment. We carried the lessons learned, the memories cherished, and the love shared deep within our souls. And as we turned the last page, we knew that the journey of love would continue in new and unexpected ways, forever illuminating our lives with its enduring magic.

The love of their lives, their wives, became invaluable pillars of support and inspiration after they entered the sacred bond of marriage. Their partners played a pivotal role in helping them remain focused on their goals and achieve success. The characters in these stories expressed profound gratitude towards their wives for their unwavering support and remained committed to staying focused on their respective paths.

On the journey of life, the love and encouragement from their spouses acted as a constant reminder of their potential and capabilities. Through the highs and lows, their wives stood by their sides, providing the strength and stability needed to overcome challenges. They offered guidance, believed in their dreams, and served as a sounding board for their ideas and aspirations.

The characters recognized that the unwavering support of their wives helped them maintain focus amidst distractions. Their partners created an environment conducive to growth, fostering a sense of purpose and determination. With their wives by their sides, they were able to persevere through obstacles and keep their eyes on the prize.

Gratitude filled their hearts as they acknowledged the impact their wives had on their success. They remained deeply appreciative of the love, sacrifices, and understanding their partners brought into their lives. The characters understood that their accomplishments were not solely due to their individual efforts but were also a testament to the love and support they received from their wives.

With their wives as their steadfast supporters, they remained committed to staying focused on their journeys. They recognized the importance of maintaining balance in their personal and professional lives, relying on their partners for guidance, strength, and unwavering belief.

The characters celebrated the power of partnership and the profound influence their wives had on their overall well-being. They understood that success was not merely measured by professional achievements but by the love and harmony they shared with their life partners.

Gratitude became a constant companion as they navigated the complexities of life hand in hand with their wives. Through thick and thin, they held onto the love and support that fueled their ambitions, ensuring that their focus remained steadfast, unwavering, and aligned with their shared vision of a fulfilling and purposeful life.

In the end, they embraced the understanding that success was not solely an individual pursuit but a collaborative effort, with their wives as their guiding lights. Together, they remained focused, driven, and grateful for the love and support they found within the sanctuary of their marriage.

Remaining focused and working diligently towards personal goals is indeed a powerful approach to life. It allows individuals to prioritize their own growth, development, and achievements. By staying committed to their aspirations, individuals can demonstrate their resilience, determination, and ability to overcome challenges.

Choosing to focus on personal success can serve as a form of self-empowerment and can be seen as a powerful response to adversity or setbacks. It enables individuals to channel their energy into productive endeavors, striving to achieve their dreams and aspirations. This dedication to personal growth can become a driving force, propelling individuals forward even in the face of obstacles or doubters.

The pursuit of personal success as a way to prove oneself can be a motivating factor for many individuals. It becomes a means of demonstrating one's abilities, proving doubters wrong, and validating one's self-worth. By dedicating themselves to their goals and consistently working towards them, individuals can showcase their capabilities and accomplishments, ultimately gaining a sense of fulfillment and satisfaction.

It is important to note, however, that while focusing on personal success is a worthy endeavor, it should not come at the expense of neglecting other important aspects of life. Striking a balance between personal and professional spheres, maintaining healthy relationships, and nurturing overall wellbeing are vital for long-term fulfillment and happiness.

Success, when defined holistically, can encompass various aspects of life, including personal growth, meaningful relationships, and a sense of purpose. It is the integration of these elements that allows for a well - rounded and satisfying life.

Ultimately, the decision to remain focused and work towards personal success is a personal one, driven by individual aspirations and desires. It can serve as a powerful catalyst for personal growth and empowerment, offering a path to achieving one's dreams and proving one's capabilities. By striving for personal success, individuals have the opportunity to create a fulfilling and impactful life, becoming the best version of themselves in the process.

There is also an important perspective. While it can be challenging to forget a first love, it is crucial to remember that there are other meaningful relationships in our lives that deserve our attention and love. Our family members, such as our parents, siblings, and others, have been there for us throughout our journey, offering their support, care, and love.

During times of heartbreak or loss, it is essential to lean on these relationships for strength and solace. Our family members can provide comfort, understanding, and a sense of belonging. They have been a constant presence in our lives, supporting us through both triumphs and tribulations.

It is important to cherish and nurture these relationships, as they offer us a sense of belonging and a support system that can guide us through difficult times.

Our family members have a deep connection with us and want to see us thrive, succeed, and be happy. They can provide us with the love and encouragement we need to heal and move forward from lost love.

It is vital to remember that our worth is not solely defined by our romantic relationships. We are multidimensional beings with unique talents, dreams, and relationships that extend beyond a single romantic connection. Our accomplishments, growth, and the love we give and receive from our family can be a source of immense pride and fulfillment.

Rather than dwelling on lost love, we can redirect our energy towards building stronger bonds with our family members, nurturing those relationships, and making them proud. By investing time and effort into these connections, we can experience a deep sense of love, acceptance, and support that can positively impact our lives.

So, in moments of heartache, let us lean on our family, draw strength from their love, and honor the connections we have with them. By cultivating and appreciating these relationships, we can create a sense of fulfillment and happiness, and a supportive network that will always be there for us.

The other important point to remember here is to love yourself before you love someone else. Loving oneself is crucial before seeking love from others, and it is essential to prioritize self-care and self-love. Taking care of our own well-being, both mentally and emotionally, is a foundational step towards leading a fulfilling life.

In the stories shared, the characters' journeys of self-discovery and personal growth serve as inspiration for others facing similar situations. These stories highlight the transformative power of self-love and the courage to overcome adversity.

By recognizing our own worth and embracing self-love, we develop a strong foundation of self-confidence, self-respect, and self-acceptance. This inner strength empowers us to make choices that align with our values, set healthy boundaries, and cultivate positive relationships.

When we prioritize self-love, we become more attuned to our own needs, desires, and aspirations. We learn to take care of ourselves, both physically and emotionally, and make choices that contribute to our overall well-being. By doing so, we create a solid foundation for personal growth and fulfillment.

Stories of self-transformation and self-love can inspire others to embark on their own journeys of self-discovery. They remind us that we have the power to rise above difficult circumstances and choose self-love and self-care as the driving forces in our lives. These stories offer hope, encouragement, and guidance to those seeking to prioritize their own well-being and find happiness within themselves.

It is important to remember that loving oneself is not a selfish act but a necessary one. When we prioritize self-love, we become better equipped to love and support others. By taking care of our own needs, we can show up for others in a more authentic and compassionate way.

So, let these stories be a source of inspiration for those seeking to embark on their own journey of self-love and personal growth. By loving and valuing ourselves, we can create a solid foundation for a fulfilling life and inspire others to do the same.

About The Author

The author, Sandeep Tiwari, is a director by profession in Germany. Along with his full-time job, he also has a flair for writing. He also has a few titles published under his name. He is well - traveled and has lived in many countries. He is a firm believer in Bhagwat Geeta and the wisdom in Bhagwat Geeta. He is passionate about talking to different people to understand their lives and also has a flair for luxury cars.